GANGLAND CARTEL 2

Romell Tukes

Lock Down Publications and Ca$h
Presents

GANGLAND CARTEL 2

A Novel by *Romell Tukes*

Romell Tukes

Lock Down Publications
P.O. Box 944
Stockbridge, Ga 30281
www.lockdownpublications.com

Copyright 2020 Romell Tukes
Gangland Cartel 2

First Edition November 2020
Printed in the United States of America

Lock Down Publications
Like our page on Facebook: Lock Down Publications @
www.facebook.com/lockdownpublications.ldp
Cover design and layout by: **Dynasty Cover Me**
Book interior design by: **Shawn Walker**
Edited by: **Jill Alicea**

Stay Connected with Us!

Text **LOCKDOWN** to 22828 to stay up-to-date with new releases, sneak peaks, contests and more…

Thank you!

Submission Guideline.

Submit the first three chapters of your completed manuscript to ldpsubmissions@gmail.com, subject line: Your book's title. The manuscript must be in a .doc file and sent as an attachment. Document should be in Times New Roman, double spaced and in size 12 font. Also, provide your synopsis and full contact information. If sending multiple submissions, they must each be in a separate email.

Have a story but no way to send it electronically? You can still submit to LDP/Ca$h Presents. Send in the first three chapters, written or typed, of your completed manuscript to:

LDP: Submissions Dept
P.O. Box 944
Stockbridge, Ga 30281

DO NOT send original manuscript. Must be a duplicate.

Provide your synopsis and a cover letter containing your full contact information.

Thanks for considering LDP and Ca$h Presents.

Acknowledgments

First and foremost, all praises are due to Allah. Shout out to my family, my Muslim brothers behind these walls with life sentences. Shout out to all the readers and my followers; I got y'all. Shout out to Yonkers, Peeky, MV, and the whole 914. Much love to Smoke Black from Y.O., my guy CB, YB, Lingo, Smurf, Spayhoe, and Tone Touch. Also Brisco, King Hound, and Baby James. My BX-fam: Melly, BT, and Frellz. My BK-team: OG Chuck, Fila, Tom Dog, and K from Thompkin and GD Tails and Gunny. NJ niggas B.G., Beast, and Roger. Philly-OG Musa from the North. Roc from B-More.

When the teachers in school told me I'd never be shit, I laughed at them. I bet they mad now LOL. Success comes from dedication. Turn your dreams into reality. Sky's the limit. Shout out to LDP. The game is ours; big facts.

Chapter 1
Cuba, Santiago de Cuba
Years Ago in Africa

"Zeema, focus on your senses or it could be fatal," an African man yelled with a strong but low-pitched voice as PYT held her sword. She was tightly blindfolded, walking through a Zimbabwean jungle near Gweru.

Zeema was PYT's African tribal name. She also had a sister named Za'alya who was the same age as her, but they had different mothers, so they looked different.

Zeema had beautiful Arabian and Indian features and her sister Za'alya was dark-skinned with long jet black hair, but she had African features. Their father was a king in Zimbabwe. He owned many tribes. When he met PYT's mom, they had her out of wedlock, and since Omen was a citizen and her mother wasn't, PYT had to stay in the country until a certain age. Her father had bigger plans for her, and that was to train her to become an assassin.

Zeema circled a tree, waiting for her attackers. This was a big part of her training.

She heard a lighter sound as if a heavy leaf had fallen from the tree behind her. She was about to get into defense mode, but it was too late.

Za'alya hopped out of the tree with a perfect landing, pressing her sword to Zeema's neck and smiling.

Zeema swiftly swung her sword, knocking Za'alya's sword away from her neck, then she attacked her with the sword, swinging it like a pro while Za'alya blocked every hit, backpedaling in the thick jungle mud.

The sound of swords clashing and sparks flying was all that could be heard as Omen watched from a distance.

Za'alya was being backed into a tree. She had to think fast. She did a front flip over Zeema's head, landing two feet behind her, giving her some control.

Zeema ducked down as a sword weaved past her head. She did a spin drop kick, making Za'alya fall on her back. Before Zeema could even jump on top of her to finish the job, Za'alya jumped up at the speed of light.

The two continued to sword fight as if they were born enemies. The blindfold was holding Zeema back from her true skills because the sword and bow were her best weapons.

Zeema had enough of the games. She did a double spin and a full round house kick, hitting Za'alya with a powerful kick and making her stumble backwards and lose her wind. Za'alya was backed into the tree. Zeema knew she had her now, so she swung her sword into the tree with all her power.

She thought the sword went into her sister, but it went through the tree, which shocked Zeema because her sister was just there.

Zeema turned around, listening for sounds, then seconds later, she felt a sharp pain in her left upper arm from Za'alya's sword.

"Enough," their father said, stepping out of the darkness. "Take off the blindfolds," he told the both of them.

When Zeema saw that her sister had on a blindfold too, she got upset while Za'alya gave her a smirk.

"I can't wait to finish you one day," Za'alya stated.

"I'll bet," she replied as they walked to their father.

Omen was a big man with big lean muscles and tribal scarification marks all over his body.

"Where are you going? You know your punishment. Never take your senses off your opponent. You will stay out here for three days," her father said, walking out of the dark, dangerous jungle with her sister, who was laughing.

Zeema sat beside a bamboo tree, clutching her sword for dear life, listening to the hyenas cry and the lions roar. She was used to this type of treatment. She was only nine years old, but she was militant with a big heart. She planned to wait for an African dog to walk past, then she would kill it and eat it. Normally that would be a three day feast for her little tummy.

***

Cuba
Present

PYT woke up sweating from her childhood dream. She had been having a lot of them lately.

"It's okay. Calm down. You will be okay," Hagor said, patting PYT lightly on her sweaty hands.

"I see I'm still here. I want to see Rugar," PYT told Hagor as she looked out the window to see trees, a farm, and lots of land behind the mansion.

"You will today, I promise. You have been weak and unable to move due to the high-powered tranquilizer," Hagor said in her strong Cuban accent.

PYT saw Hagor's long blonde hair and beautiful face and wondered if she was a model. She seemed too perfect. If she only knew...

"I'm sorry, I don't even remember your name," PYT said, sitting up.

"It's Hagor," she stated with her bright smile.

"I just want to take a shower and get dressed. Do you have an outfit for me?" PYT asked, climbing out of bed. Not cuffed anymore, she was able to move around. She looked at her undone toes, looked at Hagor's pretty manicured toes in her heels, then back at hers.

"It's okay. I will get you right, as you New York girls say it," Hagor said.

"It's the least you can do after you kidnapped me and had me shot with elephant tranquilizers," she said, making Hagor laugh.

"I understand. But you did good. I was watching the video. You have a sharp awareness," Hagor said, walking to the closet to pick out a nice dress for her.

"You look fit. Do you work out or train?" she asked Hagor, seeing that she had a toned body.

"I used to train before I retired from a certain field I was in a long time ago. Now I train our army." Hagor placed out a nice white wrap dress, a perfect fit for PYT.

"How old are you, if you don't mind me asking? You don't look older than me," PYT said, sitting so Hagor could brush her hair in front of the large mirror on the dresser.

Hagor was 5'3" in height with a light tan complexion, bluish-green eyes, long blond hair, a youthful face, white perfect teeth, perky C-cup breasts, a flat stomach, and a round soft ass with a cuff. She was all natural and dangerous.

"I wish I was your age again. I would change a lot of things I've done. But I'm forty-nine now," Hagor said as PYT looked at her, wondering how she did it. Hagor caught her look. "Lots of water, sex, and healthy eating," she said, laughing as she got done with her hair. She let PYT take a bath so she could do her nails and makeup before Jumbo got back.

PYT sat in the bubbles, soaking her body in the big tub in the private bathroom attached to her room. The bathroom had a marble floor, gold sinks, and a glass shower with a nice view of the estate. She closed her eyes, thinking about everything she been going through: Naya's imprisonment, the nephew she just met, Rugar being shot in the head by Lil C and her thinking he was dead, her killing Lil C and his mom, and now this. Never in a million years would she imagine Rugar being affiliated with the Cuban Cartel. She heard a lot about them a while back and they were nothing to fuck with.

After her bath she got dressed and did her own toes, nails, and makeup. Now she was back to herself. She looked herself in the mirror, seeing her true beauty. Now all she needed was her king back.

Looking out her bedroom windows, she saw workers on the field picking tobacco, citrus, coffee, and beans, which was amazing to her. She didn't understand how this was a Cartel estate because she saw no security. She figured they were somewhere in the house.

Hagor came back to get PYT, informing her that Jumbo was near the pool waiting on her. Hagor was impressed at how beautiful PYT looked. She reminded her of her daughter.

The two women walked downstairs in the extremely large, empty mansion that looked like a castle.

Chapter 2

PYT sat at the glass table across from Jumbo, sipping her glass of grapefruit juice. She admired the mansion. She had never seen a house so big with so much land. It looked like it never ended. She felt as if she was out of place, but she had one thing on her mind, and that was making sure Rugar made it.

"You okay, Jasmine?" Jumbo asked, snapping her out of her daze.

"Yeah I'm good." She watched him light a cigar and then unbutton the top of his Prada shirt.

"Hagor and my maids are preparing a beautiful meal for you. I'm glad to have you with us," he said, watching the sun go down over the mountains.

"No disrespect, but I don't think I can eat right this second. I really need to see Rugar," she said as he smiled. He saw how much she really loved the young man.

"Come take a walk," he said as he stood up and extended his hand to her, helping her up. They walked past the pond to a trail leading into the farm.

"This is beautiful. How much land you have?" she asked, seeing grapevines hanging from small fences.

"Close to two hundred acres. This house been a part of my family for over 100 years. My great-grandparents were slaves here. This is where it all started."

"Wow, that's crazy," PYT said, walking past workers who paid her no mind as they worked. She and Jumbo walked deeper into the field.

"What do you grow here?" she asked, seeing workers pick more than fruit and beans

"Coco leaf and poppy seeds. They are not really picking fruit. I'm sure you wondered how your Empire had the best coke and dope in the city. Brazy and Rugar have this farm to thank," Jumbo said as PYT nodded her head, not so surprised anymore. Everything was starting to add up.

"Question: why are we here?" PYT asked, stopping.

"I will tell you, but this is serious information I'm about to give you. If you don't want no parts of it, I'll fly you back out to the States and we can act like this never happened," Jumbo stated as she thought deeply on it.

"Whatever Rugar is in, I'm in," she said as she saw an arm sticking out of the dirt

"He tried to steal, so we buried half of his arm. Sorry about that. But let me explain. Rugar's mother is my little sister. We both ran away to the States to see what life was like, and that's while our parents ran the cartel. My sister met Big Jay, his pops, and they had three kids: Brazy, Rugar, and China. Then my parents both became ill and passed. I was left to run the Cartel, but I had to get married, so I met Hagor, who was an assassin at the time trying to kill me. It's' a long story. Anyway, I took over the family. When my sister was killed, I moved back to the States to watch over her kids from a distance while Pete was there guarding me. We were close back in the day so I trusted him, plus he was their uncle," he said.

PYT listened to every word closely, thinking about everything he was saying.

"I controlled the drug trade in the USA while Hagor held down the Cartel here. Brazy is dead. Rugar is up next to take over the family business. Since he is the only kin I have left, it's already written and sealed. Me and my wife are retiring, so since China is too young and unaware of this lifestyle, you and Rugar will take our powerful position. That's about it," he said.

"This is crazy! I'm sure Rugar don't have a clue," PYT said.

"No. When he was shot, those were my men I had go pick him up in the EMS truck. I knew Lil C was back from Cali. I had eyes on him, so I knew he was coming. I had love for that kid. I trained Lil C and raised Chris. But I refused to sit back and let him kill my nephew. The night you sneaked in their window and killed them, my men was parked down the block waiting on him to come out. But there was only you," he said.

She looked shocked. She had no clue someone was watching. "Does Rugar know you're his uncle?"

"No. He believes I'm his godfather. When he came here, he was dead. My doctors brought him back to life. Then he went into a coma, which is still his condition," he said.

"What's the real reason you retiring?" she asked, wondering why he wanted to give all of this up.

"I'm getting old, and I recently found out I have prostate cancer, so before I leave this earth, I want to pass the torch to Rugar. We sent a lookalike body to the morgue and gave Rugar a closed casket funeral because I got wind the Feds was onto him," Jumbo said, walking back towards the castle.

"I'm ready to see him," PYT said.

"Okay, come on. I know your feet hurt," he said, laughing.

"Hell yeah. But where is your security? I never saw a cartel family with no protection," she said as he laughed.

"Look around again," he said.

"What? All I see is eighty workers slaving," she said.

"Correct. Those workers are all well-trained and all have weapons on them. Approximately 478,000 Cuban workers are currently self-employed. I own petroleum products, hotels out here, homes, restaurants in Latkbana, Granma, Holguin, and Villa Cilara," Jumbo stated, walking in the house.

They took an elevator to the underground hospital he had built in the house. It looked like a real hospital with long bright hallways, shiny buff floors, doctors, nurses, hospital rooms, machines, and of course, the smell.

"Is this a real hospital for people?" she asked, seeing doctors in lab coats walk past her.

"It's a real hospital. We even got a medical airlift on the roof. But it's only for my workers and family," he said, walking through double doors.

Jumbo and PYT stopped at a large glass window to see two doctors running tests on Rugar as he laid in a coma, hooked up to IVs and machines. PYT had tears rolling down her cheeks, ruining her makeup.

"It's going to be okay. Have faith. I have the best doctors from New York and Havana working on him," he said strongly as the doctors finished up.

"What's up, bossman?" a short, older white man said. He had short gray hair and was followed by a Cuban man in a blue lab coat with big glasses.

They were there to personally work on Rugar. At first, both men refused until Jumbo had their families kidnapped and beaten. Then both doctors agreed to help bring Rugar back to life. They couldn't leave the compound until Rugar was up and well. After that, they could both go home ten million dollars richer apiece.

"Update me and his soon-to-be wife - and don't upset me," Jumbo said

"Well, boss, he is still in a coma. He was really luckily the bullet missed the peripheral nerve. The tests are getting better. We believe he could make it. He may only suffer some memory loss," the Cuban doctor said

"Yeah, but he is in good health," the white doctor said, angry that the Cuban doctor was telling Jumbo bad news because he wanted to make it outta there alive with ten million dollars.

"How long could it take for him to wake up?" PYT asked softly.

"It all depends on how fast his brain cells can work together again," the Cuban doctor said.

"Can I stay down here with him please?" she asked Jumbo with glossy eyes.

"I don't think that will be a good idea," the white doctor said.

"Get her a bed, blanket, sheets, and whatever she needs. Treat her as if she was him," Jumbo said, walking off as they rushed to get her a bed, food, clothes, TV, and books.

Chapter 3
Weeks later

PYT laid in her own bed near Rugar in the hospital, watching him in his coma, overwhelmed by everything. She had no ties to the States. She knew the Empire and Naya were pissed. She couldn't believe she and Rugar were being given an opportunity to run a cartel because she was a trained killer and he was a gangbanger from Harlem.

She hadn't left his side since she saw him in his coma. She refused to go anywhere. She showered down there, ate, and watched the doctors give him meds in the IVs and make sure he was hydrated.

She was sound asleep under her thick cotton sheets until she heard loud beeping, which wasn't normal. She jumped up in her pajamas with her pistol, alarmed, as if it was an attack. The machines were going crazy. She thought he was dying.

"Doc, Doc, Doc, help!" she yelled.

Four doctors were already rushing into the room. Rugar's body was shaking while they shocked his chest and pumped his heart until his eyes came open. When PYT saw this, she started to cry. He was alive.

"Thank you, Doc." She breathed a heavy sigh of relief.

"He is alive, but we don't know his condition as of yet. We have to run some tests. But our biggest fear is that he will have memory loss," he said.

"How long until you are able to find out?" she asked, hoping that wasn't the case.

"When he fully wakes up. He's sleeping now and he is under a lot of meds," he said.

"Okay, thanks. But I need some of that to take home with me," she said.

"Of course, why not? But it's illegal in the States," he said, walking off and laughing, thinking about that ten million dollars promised to him.

***

Hagor and PYT stood in a small field on the other side of the castle. The small dirt field was packed with workout equipment: climbing walls, robes, tires, sand bags, swords, barbed wire, and a bow and gun range.

There was a large group of males and females dressed in army gear in lines, training hard as they did every day.

PYT watched a fighting match with a bound woman fighting off two male attackers, and she was kicking their asses.

"Damn, who is she?" PYT asked as she saw the girl, who was no older than eighteen years old, break one of their arms and slam the other male, pointing her gun to his head.

"That's my daughter. She normally trains the army at the other compound, but she is our best shooter and fighter. She is only seventeen," Hagor stated, feeling the tropical wind.

"She's beautiful. And you and Jumbo have kids? Wow," PYT said as gunshots could be heard from the gun range.

"No. After I killed her father, Miguel Bermudez, I was hired to kill Jumbo, but I fell in love with him," Hagor said, smiling, thinking how crazy it sounded. "Would you like to meet Savannah?" Hagor called her daughter's name, getting her attention.

"Hagor, hi," her daughter said, approaching them as her mom gave her a disapproving look. She disliked Savannah calling her by her real name.

Savannah was beautiful. She was her mom's twin, but her hair hung down to her thighs, so she always wrapped it up. She was light-skinned, 5'5", petite, with small B-cup breasts, thick lips, a small butt, hazel almond-shaped eyes, and she had facial piercings.

"This is Jasmine, Rugar's girlfriend. They're going to be the ones taking over," she told her daughter, who looked PYT up and down with envy.

"Nice to meet you," Savannah said in bad English.

"Same to you. Keep up the good work," PYT said.

"Mom, I had no idea American girls were beautiful," Savannah said in Spanish to her mom.

"Some of us are," PYT replied in Spanish, shocking both of them.

"You speak Spanish?" Hagor asked.

"Of course," she said in Spanish as Savannah frowned.

"I have to go. I have my own estate miles away. I'm rarely up here. But I hope to see you again," Savannah said in Spanish with a fake smile before walking off.

"She is very pretty and militant," PYT said as they walked around.

"Yes she is. She was supposed to take over the family, but she is too young, and she was pleased you and Rugar were chosen."

"Oh," she replied, knowing Savannah had a dislike for her already, so this was a surprise to hear.

"Yeah, she loves to kill. That's her field, just like her uncle, who is the best assassin to come outta Central America. They call him Black Mist in English," Hagor said, speaking proudly of him.

"I heard of him," PYT said, knowing who he was because he stole a couple of her jobs in the Caribbean.

"Yes, he speaks highly of you, dear. That's how I heard of you," she said.

The rest of the evening, Hagor gave PYT a rundown from A to Z about the cartel and the other dangerous families and the business aspect of it.

***

Days later…

PYT sat by Rugar's bed frame, praying like a nun asking for forgiveness with her eyes closed.

"Since when you started praying?" Rugar asked her, saying his first words since he came out his coma

"Oh my God, you know who I am!" she said, excited.

"Of course I do, Tamika," he said softly.

"Who the fuck is Tamika? You really don't remember me?" PYT asked, face to face with him.

"You got older, Tamika. Where is our dog?" Rugar said as PYT sat down, about to cry because she knew he had lost his memory.

"It's okay, Jasmine, I know who you are. I love you," he said as she hugged him.

"Boy, don't ever do that," she said, laughing. He had scared her. "Don't talk too much. I don't want you to hurt yourself. Are you okay?" she asked.

"I'm good. I got a headache. Where are we? What happened?" he asked seriously, looking around the unfamiliar room.

"We're in Cuba. Jumbo saved your life, baby, after Lil C tried to kill you. Baby, he shot you in the head," she said sadly.

"I'ma kill that bitch nigga," he said with pain in his face.

"I already killed him and his mother," she said.

"What? How was you in Atlanta and how did we get here? Jumbo brought us here…but why? Do you have a gun?"

"Here, baby," she said, handing him her pistol. "It's a long story, but I'ma start from the bottom." It took her over an hour to explain everything.

"Damn, this is crazy. Me and you running a cartel family? What about the Empire? And the cartel is a whole 'nother level, babe. What do you want to do?" he asked.

"Whatever my future husband wants to do," she replied.

The two talked for hours until it was time for his medicine, which put him to sleep in minutes. Jumbo and Hagor came down, happy to hear he was well and healthy.

Chapter 4
Weeks later

The past couple of weeks had been a healing process for Rugar. He was slowly gaining his strength back.

Spending hours with Jumbo and finding out he was his real uncle overwhelmed him. He saw pictures of his mom and Jumbo as kids. As a kid he used to wonder why Uncle P never told him about his mom's side of the family. He thought she was an orphan.

Rugar was doing four to six hours of therapy a day, everything from walking, running, weights, cardio, and swimming. He had lost a lot of blood being shot six times in the upper torso so he had lost a lot of muscle mass, but he still had his cuts and chiseled frame.

He was doing laps inside the underground indoor pool area. He had become a pro at swimming. He used to be scared to swim.

"He is a good swimmer," Hagor told PYT as both women sat by the pool in bikinis, showing off their amazing, perfect bodies.

"Yeah. I'm just glad he's back," PYT said as she watched Jumbo come down, smoking a cigar and wearing flip flops and shorts.

"Rugar, come to my office!" Jumbo yelled, walking close to the women. "Ladies, going for a swim, I see," he said, walking past them.

Rugar climbed out of the pool shirtless, showing off his six pack and dick print in his shorts as he wrapped a towel around his waist and threw on a tank top over his tatted body

"I beat last week's record. I'm going for a run around the compound in an hour. Y'all want to join me?" he asked them both as he approached them, smiling.

"Sure," both of them said from behind their designer Fendi shades with their pussies soaking wet - and not from their swim.

"So did you two come up with a decision?" Hagor asked, breaking the tension as Rugar walked inside.

"I'm just waiting on him. He's still healing and trying to get his thoughts together."

"I understand. But I assume you didn't tell him about Jumbo's cancer?" she asked PYT.

"No. I think it would be better if Jumbo did that," she said.

"It makes sense, but as I told you, we have meetings once a year, and this year's meeting is soon with all the families," Hagor said.

"Okay. I'm sure he'll be ready soon," PYT said, thinking about how dramatically her life would change if Rugar accepted this new position. "Are you okay with retiring too? I know you have no choice because of the situation," PYT asked.

"I'm married to my husband, not the power, so I'm okay with it. I just hope Jumbo can beat this cancer. But the docs all say it's too late," Hagor said as the white and Cuban doctors walked into the pool area with smiles.

"Ms. Hagor, is Jumbo around? We're trying to get the ten million and go home. We did our job here with the kid," the white doctor from New York said.

"Oh, yes, how would you like it? Cash or check?" Hagor asked, standing up. Both men looked at her camel toe and flat stomach and nice breasts.

"Cash is perfect," the Cuban doctor said as Hagor walked past them with her G-string swallowed by her ass cheeks. Her ass moved with every strut. Even PYT was surprised at how big and perfect her ass was. She had the body of a stripper.

Hagor came out from the back with a cotton robe on and a gun in her hand. She killed both doctors. Their bodies fell in the pool, turning the clear water dark red.

"How about we go into town to do a little food shopping and prepare a meal tonight for everyone?" she said.

"Sure," PYT said, putting on her robe, not really impressed by the little scene. She stood to go upstairs as workers entered to clean up the bodies and make them disappear.

***

Rugar took a quick shower and put on his tailor-made suit. Jumbo had measured him and given it to him along with forty others. He was now twenty-one years old. He was shocked at how fast time flew. He remembered it was yesterday when he and his best friend Montana were running the streets for a name, but now Montana was dead.

Rugar didn't know if he was truly ready to take over one of the most powerful cartel families, but then again, he thought he wasn't ready to run the Empire after Brazy's death, and he did that with an iron fist.

Rugar walked to Jumbo's office down the hall. The door was open when he knocked.

"Come in, kid," Jumbo said while he was on the phone behind a large oak desk. The office was medium-sized with cabinets, TV monitors for the cameras, laptops, guns, and photos of his grandparents on the designer wallpaper made in France.

"Nephew, have a seat," Jumbo said, smiling with his hand on his chin as if he was in deep thought. "I want to tell you something. I'ma be honest with you, kid. I'm dying of cancer and I don't have long to live. That's why I'm really stepping down and why I need you to step up. I know it's short notice, but don't worry about me," Jumbo said, coughing after a cigar drag.

"You okay?" Rugar asked, feeling sad for his uncle. He had just really started to build a bond with him.

"I'm good, kid," Jumbo said.

"How come you never had kids?" Rugar asked.

"I had a son a long time ago. There was a cartel war with the Portuguese Cartel. They kidnapped my son and sent his six-year-old body to me after they killed him, then we murdered their whole bloodline," Jumbo said.

"Sorry."

"It's the life of this cartel. One mistake in this shit can cost you your life and your family their lives. These are dangerous people, Rugar. They're heartless. That's why I kept Breezy, you, and China in the dark - to protect y'all," Jumbo said honestly.

"I live by the Omerta code, so I'm willing to accept everything that comes with this life," Rugar said, thinking about Jumbo dying of cancer.

"Does this mean you're ready to join the family?" Jumbo asked.

"I been doing a lot of thinking, and I'm ready."

"Please understand what you're about to get into. You're about to deal with the world's deadliest cartel families," Jumbo said.

"I'll be ready for the meeting next month," Rugar said.

"Okay, excellent. I just got off the phone with the Mexican Cartel, who are connected to the FBI. You was wanted for questioning for murders, but there was no case. Everybody thinks you're dead, Rugar. They're working on clearing you as we speak. But wait awhile until you got back to the States. To be honest, I think it's best you let PYT run the Empire and drug trade. All of them dudes are solid. I got eyes everywhere," Jumbo said.

"Okay, but am I going to be the only black nigga in the cartel?" Rugar asked with a laugh.

"No, you won't, but you will be the youngest besides Katie, who runs the UK Cartel. Watch out for her, kid, really. She's pretty, young, poisonous, and deadly. Welcome to the family. You was born into this shit, unlike most," Jumbo said, cutting a Cuban cigar and passing it to the new don.

"Thanks," he said, lighting it.

"Cuba has the best cigars in the world," Jumbo said.

"I have heard," Rugar said, choking as Jumbo laughed.

"Listen, always keep this house. Pass it down our bloodline."

"Okay, but what about your wife?" Rugar asked.

"Don't worry about her. She got six mansions and she's rich forever. But still, keep an eye on her," he said.

"I plan to propose to Jasmine tonight. I even went out to get the biggest diamond ring with Hagor the other morning," Rugar said, showing him the large rock.

"Damn, she deserves it, kid. She's loyal. There wasn't one day she wasn't by your side. She's a good woman. But be careful. She is a very deadly woman. I heard of her before I met her. Be smart and be a good husband," Jumbo said seriously.

Chapter 5

After Jumbo said the prayer in Spanish, everybody began eating the large meal. The women had made everything: wild rice, beans, pork, salads, fresh veggies, fruits, chicken, turkey, and seafood.

"I'm very glad to have my family here with me," Jumbo said, eating his seafood salad.

"I'm glad to be here. It's an honor," Rugar said, watching Savannah play in her food with her head down. Today was the first day he met her and he got a bad vibe from her.

"Of course, kid. I'm glad you made the choice to carry the torch because if you would have said no, we would have had to kill you," Jumbo said, laughing but serious.

"Congratulations to the both of you. I'm sure the both of you deserve your crowns - isn't that right, Savannah Suarez?" said Hagor, looking at her daughter, who was in another world.

"Yes, Mom. I'm very happy for them," Savannah said, giving off a fake smile. She wasn't impressed at all with the two. They didn't look too much like killers or powerful enough to run a cartel. She heard so much about the deadliest assassin in Africa, only to get a Miss America or prom queen. At the end of the day, she didn't give a fuck about them or Hagor, Jumbo, and the cartel. She wanted her whole own Empire for herself.

"Excuse me. I have to use the lady's room," Savannah said in Spanish as she stood up from the table in a beautiful red dress, showing her small breasts in her Giambattista Valli high-low tulle dress.

Hagor shook her head at her daughter. She had no clue what was going on with her, but she would find out soon.

Rugar stood up to make an announcement at the large table. "I would like to think my uncle, his beautiful wife, and her beautiful daughter for their hospitality," Rugar said.

As Savannah walked back into the room, she was caught off-guard by him referring to her as beautiful.

"Today will not only be a new start of my life within the car-tel, but I'm hoping also with marriage," he said, looking at PYT.

Savannah looked confused, hoping he wasn't about to pop the question. She thought he was cute, but she would never tell anybody. Even though she was still a virgin, she wouldn't mind sucking his dick and letting him cum in her mouth.

"Will you marry me?" Rugar asked, getting on his knees in front of PYT with a huge ring in his hand.

"Yes…yesss!" she said, covering her mouth.

Everybody was clapping except Savannah, who stood on the wall with jealousy.

The rest of the night went smoothly. Everybody enjoyed themselves, planning for the big wedding.

***

Two weeks later

Rugar stood in the guest room staring at himself in the mirror as he fixed the tie on his Marc Jacob custom-made suit. He had been waiting a while to marry PYT and the day had finally arrived. He felt as if he dreams were unfolding before his eyes life was moving fast since he came out the coma.

Rugar stared at his clean cut handsome face, thinking about everybody he lost: Hand, Brazy, Uncle P, and Montana. He knew if Brazy was alive he would tell him money, power, and respect are the keys to life.

There was a light knock at the door. Jumbo stood there in an all-black tuxedo, looking clean and healthy.

"Today is your day. We have a lot of important people in the area today. I ordered your white Henny and Cirôc, and as you asked, we have soul food and Latin food," Jumbo stated.

"How I look?" Rugar asked.

"Like your father," Jumbo said with a chuckle.

"I'll take that as a compliment. But I'm truly becoming a man now," Rugar said, smiling.

"Let me tell you something. A man can never become a full man until he creates a family and take cares of them. Follow the code of honor and you will make it far, kid. I love you," Jumbo said strongly as he kissed him on his forehead.

***

The wedding was being held in the backyard area behind the guest house, which was large and spacious.

PYT and Hagor spent two days setting up the wedding. There were going to be a lot of powerful people there, so they had to do it big.

The sun was hiding under the thick clouds as the skyline stood out brightly and there was a nice windy breeze.

The DJ had been flown in first class from Canada. The priest waited at the altar with Rugar. The best man and all four hundred guests were sitting in their assigned seats listen to the Jagged Edge song "Let's Get Married" play loudly. Most of the guest bopped their heads off beat, not knowing the song, but they liked the rhythms.

Seconds later, PYT walked down the aisle in an all-white Alexandra McQueen gown so long it could drag for half a block.

All the cartel families in the audience knew of Jumbo and Hagor's retirement, but today was the first time they laid eyes on the beautiful young couple taking over.

Hagor was PYT's bridesmaid. She looked amazing in a white Ferragamo dress that hugged her curves.

Standing now face to face with Rugar, PYT's stomach got bubbly. He grabbed her hands while the priest began the ceremony. The priest was known throughout Cuba. He spoke English and Spanish well. After he read them their oaths, he told them they could read each other their vows. Once they exchanged vows and kissed, the crowd went crazy in all types of different languages.

The night was full of fun music, drinks, food, dancing, and lots of cigar smoking. Jumbo entertained his guests while PYT cut the seven foot cake and smashed some in Rugar's face. They ran off as the guests enjoyed the white chocolate cake.

"I see you know how to pick them," Juda of the Egyptian Cartel stated, surrounded by his goons and talking to Jumbo. Juda was dark-skinned with dark hair. He also had several wives from Thebes, Nobia, and Itjtawy.

"Yes I do, my friend. That's the only reason you're alive," Jumbo said honestly. He had saved Juda's life from the hand of an Egyptian king before Jumbo killed him and he had let Juda take over his country's cartel trade.

"Memories. But I have to go. I'll see you for the meeting, my man," Juda said in his strong accent.

Jumbo continued to speak to other guests while everybody watched PYT and Rugar dance as if they were on *Dancing with the Stars*.

Hagor walked over to Jumbo, who was talking to Prince Abdulla Akbar from Riyadh, Saudi Arabia.

"Excuse me, gentlemen. Can I have my lovely husband for a second?" she asked.

"Pardon me, gentlemen. Enjoy your evening. I'll see you soon. I think my wife wants a dance," Jumbo said, walking off as Hagor led him to the dance floor to get a slow dance next to the couple of the day.

Chapter 6

Rugar and PYT were on their honeymoon in Las Tunas, Cuba in a fancy hotel that sat on the beach with crystal clear water and white sand. The hotel room had one large room with a door opening to the beach and came with a personal chef, a bar, and an all-white living room with white curtains.

The two made love all night until the sun came up. It was the craziest sexual healing the two ever did. It was amazing.

Rugar loved seeing his wife asleep because it was so peaceful. PYT was unlike most women whose wigs and makeup were all off in the morning and they looked like Freddy Kruger. He went to stand on the balcony in his silk Louis Vuitton rope, clearing his thought process as he heard his wife move around.

"Good morning, my dear," PYT said, getting out of the bed naked, showing her phat little pussy and nice breasts as she donned an Attico silk robe.

"Whats popping? You brush your gums?" he asked as she wrapped her hands around his abs.

"You love my stanky breath, nigga, don't front," she said, hugging his back. "You okay?"

"I'm sorry, just a little hesitant about sending you back to the States and with the responsibilities I left behind. Not to mention all the enemies I could have still have out there," Rugar said, turning around and looking in her gray eyes

"There's no need to hesitate. We still got the Empire, so we still got an army, and now with the Cartel behind us, our shit can be untouchable. Don't let your paranoid views deter you from your main priorities. We run a big nation." PYT said firmly

"You right. I was just overanalyzing the situation. I'm sure you will be okay and I'm sure I'll be clear soon," he said.

"Don't worry. It will work We got each other, babe," she said, kissing him passionately

"It's no alternative to failure. We about to take over the streets again," he said as they went to make love again.

***

Days later

"All the cartel families are behind them double doors. Today you become a man in the underworld society. Welcome to the Cartel, kid. Present a strong reputation and people will respect you. Intimidate the weak and people will fear you. Know who you dealing with before you affiliate yourself with any of them. It could be successful or deadly," Jumbo stated.

"I understand," he replied.

"These cartel families are the most dangerous, smartest, successful, wealthiest, and unpredictable men and women you will ever meet," Jumbo said as Rugar took a deep breath.

Jumbo opened the wide double doors and Rugar stepped inside in a Louis Vuitton three piece suit. He saw the room get so quiet a pen dropping would sound like a bomb going off.

There was a long table in the large room with twenty-five seats filled with powerful men and women. PYT sat in the front near Hagor while Rugar took his seat near Jumbo, who sat at the head of the table because the Cuban Cartel was the head of all the families. They supplied all the drugs.

"Good afternoon, ladies and gentlemen," Jumbo said, looking around the room. Everybody had glasses of wine and Louis Vuitton 13 champagne.

"As you all know, I'm Jumbo and I run the Cuban Cartel, and my wife Hagor is my other half. She controls Cuba while I control the U.S. jurisdictions. Due to only having a meeting once a year, I haven't had the chance to tell everyone here that I will be retiring - me and my wife," Jumbo said with a cough.

Jumbo saw all the devastated and furious looks around the room. So many people had questions.

"This young man here is Rugar, my nephew, my bloodline and the new leader of this family. He is going to take my place today. I can assure you all he is well-trained, business oriented, and he took his oath within the family, so the code and rules are already established. Please give him a chance for me. We still follow the protocol of this organization, but he is the one; trust me. This is his wife PYT. She will take Hagor's seat," he said as a couple of people choked upon hearing the famous assassin's name.

"Guess a lot of you heard of her. I'm dying of cancer. I served this family well and it was my privilege, but I can assure you all, they will carry the torch. Do we have any concerns or worries?" Jumbo asked in a serious tone.

Whoever was to disagree with the boss would most likely be denied and outvoted, and that could lead to a war, since Jumbo supplied all of them.

"I have a concern. I'm not going against your judgment at all, Jumbo, but will the drug trade remain the same?" the Brazzo Cartel family boss asked.

"No worries. You have my word, because money and power is why we're all here, and it is the reason why my grandparents started this shit," Jumbo stated. "Rugar and Jasmine, come take your seat as the new leaders of the Cartel," Jumbo said as the whole room began clapping loudly.

"Thank you very much. First, me and my wife would like to thank everyone for giving me a chance. I can assure you all, the drug trade will get better and there will be lower prices. I've done a lot of research on all twenty-four families in this room, from Carlos De Rosa of Mexico, the Inez Cartel in the UK, the Mulberry Cartel in Haiti, the Juda Cartel in Egypt, and the Akbar Cartel in the Middle East stealing oil," Rugar said, making everyone laugh as he named many families in the room while most of them didn't even remember his name. "Me and my wife have set up new accounts for you all to transfer and wire money monthly after your shipments land, and I will be dropping the prices as of today. I have some shit in the making that will make your countries go crazy. Thank you for opening your arms to me and my wife," he said, ending the meeting.

Everybody talked, drank, laughed, and spoke to Rugar and PYT, excited about the new prices. They had forgotten about Jumbo and Hagor already.

Chapter 7
FBI Headquarters, NY

"Sir, the NYPD's best detectives and I have been trying to solve and understand this case for over a year. The gang war left so many bodies that we honestly didn't know where to start. I've been investigating these thugs and there is a lot of shit that is not adding up, but I feel like I'm getting close. I believe these wars are behind something else," Agent Morris said. He had been Pelzo's partner in the FBI before he retired months ago.

Morris was born and raised in New Jersey. He had been a part of the FBI for ten years. He was forty years old, handsome, African-American, and a musclehead. He had done twelve years in the Navy SEAL Special Ops, so he was well-trained.

Agent Morris was sitting in front of his boss like a kid in a principal's office who was in trouble while Agent Lopez typed in his email, paying him no mind.

"Morris, let me make myself clearer than I have ever been in my whole twenty-five year career," Agent Lopez said, lifting his head.

"Yes sir," he replied.

"This is a cold case. It's closed, I don't give a fuck if Biggie or 2pac pops up from the grave with Blue's Clues," Lopez told his agent.

"Bur sir, over seventy young men were wounded or gunned down in the last two years across our city behind this," he said, hoping his boss would see his logic.

The captain gave off a little laugh as he leaned back in his chair. "People lose their lives every day in this country and all over the world, if you haven't noticed. Did you read the newspaper this morning? A family was tied up, robbed, and killed by a homeless man in Manhattan. Go work on that case. If you want to analyze gang activity, you should have been a part of the gang unit. If you want to find goldfish instead of sharks, you should have been a detective. If I ever hear about this case again, your job will be on the line. Do you understand? Good. Now get out," Lopez stated.

"Yes sir," Agent Morris said, shocked.

"Agent, go buy some pussy. You look stressed," Lopez said as Morris walked out of his office pissed.

Joseph Lopez was born in Mexico. His family was full of very powerful and wealthy people connected to the government. He refused to let Morris fuck up his operation. Lopez lit a cigar, pulled out his private cell phone, and made a call with a smirk.

***

Bronx, NY

"You telling me niggas hit two of my spots in two weeks and nobody knows shit, Blood?" Red Hat asked Murder as he sat on the hood of his new red Maserati coupe in front of Castle Hill projects.

"Homie, they killed everybody in the crib, bro."

"How much they took, Blood?" Red Hat said, trying not to show his true anger.

"That's the crazy part. They ain't take shit," Murder said, confusing him.

"What? Either a nigga trying to send a message or play games. Look, find out if there is some new heavy hitters in the town. Sometimes money is the root to all evil," Red Hat stated, in deep thought.

"Say no more, my G," Murder said to his best friend.

"Guess who about to come back to town?"

"I don't know, but I hope it's some snow bunnies, because Easter is near."

"Far from the Easter bunny, Blood. PYT back," Red Hat said, turning on his quite engine

"I know she sick about the big homie passing."

"Facts. But nobody deserves son's throne within the Empire more than her," Red Hat said as he pulled off into the busy Bronx streets. Driving down the blocks, he saw NYPD officers, gang-bangers, drug dealers, and school kids. These were the streets he knew since he was a kid.

He made his way to Melrose projects to holla at his young gunners, who were kicking off twenty keys every two days. Red Hat wondered who was knocking off his men. He could only figure out one group of individuals who would have the nuts to do this and that was the Crips, but since Lil C's death, they had been out of the picture. He was so happy PYT was on her way back. He knew she was hurt about Rugar, but he knew she was very strong.

When Rugar's death hit the city, there was a four month drought. Luckily, Bam Bam from Brooklyn had a connect in Miami who was looking out.

***

Brooklyn, NY

Bam Bam's grill was the only thing shining in the dark room in East New York in the basement of an abandoned house.

Ty was fucked up, barely breathing. His hands and ankles were tied to a chair while twenty goons surrounded him.

"How is it that you're the only nigga alive and niggas killed six of my niggas?" Bam Bam yelled. He had been trying to figure out who would run in his trap to kill his goons and leave thirty-six keys of coke behind.

"I was in the bathroom shitting blood when I heard gunshots. I got my burner and came out busting, but they was gone, Blood," Ty said, lying. When he was taking a shit, he heard shots and jumped out the window and took off.

"I believe you," Bam Bam said, laughing before he shot Ty in the side of the head eight times.

"Clean this up after someone takes a shit on him, since this bitch-ass nigga likes to take shits. Find out who ran up in my spot!" Bam Bam said, leaving the building with five niggas behind him.

Bam Bam had Brooklyn on lock with the drug trade thanks to his Miami plug. He had just gotten a text saying the Princess was on her way back. He had no clue where PYT had been. It was like she had disappeared without a trace. He was upset with her, and she had better explain herself to the Empire or else she was food.

Chapter 8
Miami, FL

China was face down, ass up in her white cotton Gucci sheets, squeezing her pillows while moaning and screaming as Pressure pulled her hair lightly, fucking her from behind.

"Uggghh, yesss, daddy!" China yelled as he went deeper in her warm, super wet, super tight pussy.

Pressure grabbed her wide hips and held on tightly as she started throwing her ass back on his dick, making it clap and move in the motion of a wave. She was taking all 9 ½ inches like a pro.

"Ohhh shittt, nigga! Ugggh!" she moaned, trying to run from the dick as he pounded away and she came on his dick with her creamy cum. He kept going until he came in her for the fifth time in three hours.

The two were exhausted. Every time they fucked, they pushed it to their limits.

"Damn, boo, I guess that makes up for you not being here last night," she said, putting on her panties over her jiggly ass and throwing on her tank top

"I'm sorry, shawty, I was in Atlanta. You know how shit gets down there," he said smoothly as he got dressed in a Balmain outfit.

China and Pressure had been together for about eight months. The two were head over heels for each other. They even got each other's names tatted.

China met Pressure through Naya's boyfriend Ronell. The two went to visit and he told her he had someone who would fit her perfectly: his right hand man Pressure. The two met, went on a couple of dates, and it was history. He was her type: tall, lean and fit, with hazel eyes, long neat dreads, white teeth, tattooed light skin, and his dick game was crazy.

China was still in college and focused. Since her brother's life was different, she felt alone and with her uncle dead, she was. Luckily PYT left her a big will she could live off. But money couldn't replace lost ones that were dear to her. She thought about

Rugar every day and talked so much about him that people thought he was a household name.

"I'ma see you later, babe," he said, kissing her on her soft lips while she worked on her laptop, then he walked out.

Malcom Washington Pri Vert, a.k.a. Pressure, was three years older than China. He had recently done a five year Fed bid for trafficking drugs and his co-defendant was Ronell, who also did five years. He was born in Verrettes, Haiti, but when his father was murdered by local thieves, his mother moved to Carol City, Miami.

Pressure had made a name for himself in the streets. He was a dangerous killer and well-respected throughout Miami and Atlanta. They were seeing major paper in New York, Philly, and D.C. thanks to Pressure. Ronell had built his empire from the ground up, thanks to Naya fronting him bricks. He told China this street shit was his life and she accepted it because it was all she knew as well.

***

North Miami
Club Smokes

Ronell sat in his office behind his small desk, going over some documents his lawyer had faxed him earlier concerning the new club he just opened in Atlanta.

He took a break and went to the bar in his office to pour himself a drink while he looked out the window towards the partygoers dancing, smoking, drinking, popping bottles, and enjoying life.

The office had mink rugs, handcrafted tables from France, and tiger heads hanging from the wall, at least four of them killed by hunters.

He sat back down and though back to when he was stripping for four months before he met Naya so he could get on his feet and get back in the dope game, because he came home from prison fucked up. He had two co-defendants: Pressure, and Big Joey, who ratted and was never heard from again. He was hiding out.

Naya changed his life. Without her, he wouldn't have anything, and she was the only woman he ever fell in love with. When she got arrested and was labeled queenpin, he was shocked, mad, and depressed. The night they had sex was still fresh on his mind. He never had pussy so good. She had stalker pussy.

He used to visit her daily in New York. He was there for her trial, and when she was sentenced to life, he was still there. She was shipped to a female max in Florida so he was able to visit her every weekend, and he did just that every Saturday morning at 9 a.m.

Naya made him stop stripping and she gave him so many bricks he could build a mansion, as long as he was loyal to her and their friendship, because she really cared for him.

Ronell took over the streets, rebuilt a powerful army, bought businesses, and he controlled the inner city drug trade in Miami. Naya told him to find a connect if he ever ran out and he did in his club one night, a beautiful white girl named Katie from the UK. Once the two talked, it was over. Katie had heard a lot about the handsome prince of the city. The two had sex one time and after that, it was all business. Katie was a big freak and dangerous. He woke up tied up with a knife to his neck. She warned him if he ever crossed her, he would die. He let it slide because he needed a plug and her head game was grade-A.

The business was booming, thanks to Katie's cartel Empire. Ronell had to admit it was amazing product.

Pressure walked in his office without knocking.

"Damn, you can't knock? You ain't learn yet. You want another knife put in you, I see," Ronell said, annoyed

"Yeah, the first nigga dead who stabbed me. You can be the second. But anyway, I'm heading to D.C. to holla at Yangin and Squirt. I'm just checking in before I bounce," Pressure said, walking to the bar to drink Henny out of the bottle, as always.

Chapter 9
Long Island, NY

Red Hat, Bam Bam, Big Smokey, and Bullet all sat in a new low-key location in L.I. near a railroad track. It was an abandoned factory Bullet owned.

"I guess we all got the text from the walking dead. How the fuck she get my number anyway? Word, son," Big Smokey stated, sitting at a round table with the Empire.

The truth was, all four of them were somewhat upset. PYT had taken off without a trace - no letters, calls, messages, nothing. They didn't even know if she was alive. Once Rugar was killed, everything went downhill, and for her to leave them with Naya in jail left a salty taste in their mouths.

"I hope she got a legit excuse, because I'm real live irritated," Bam Bam said, mad because he had to send his men to Miami twice a week and he was taking risks.

"I'm sure our African princess won't devastate us. Has she yet?" Red Hat said, making everyone shut up.

Everyone heard a loud sports bike race into the lot with five all-black SUV trucks behind it

"Damn, we got company, Bloods," Bam Bam said, looking out the smashed windows and pulling out two pistols while everybody else picked up their assault rifles.

Nobody came with security to meetings anymore since Rugar's death, so they came strapped up and alone.

"That's not the boys, Blood. Y'all wilding," Red Hat said, sitting down when he saw the jacket and helmet pulled off.

***

PYT hopped off the bike, taking off her leather coat and helmet, laying her ponytail down. She walked into the warehouse like a diva as twenty Spanish niggas with weapons surrounded the building.

"Looks like you got a tan on the beach, Blood. How was your vacation?" Bullet asked her sarcastically as she approached the table that held the four deadliest men in New York.

"Hello, gentlemen. First, I just want to say I'm sorry for my absence, but my reason will make you understand," she said as she looked all of them in their eyes.

"We was worried sick about you, ma. After Rugar got killed, we put an APB out on you," Red Hat said while staring at the biggest diamond ring he ever saw on her hand. He couldn't picture her moving on so fast and marrying someone.

"Let me explain," she said.

"Please do, Barbie doll," Big Smokey said.

"Don't push it, nigga. But listen, please. I was kidnapped after I killed Lil C and his mom," she said.

"Fuck, I knew it! Who?" Red Hat shouted.

"It's okay. Listen, I was drugged and I woke up in Cuba with the Cartel," she said.

"Why would they kidnap you? I don't get it at all," Bullet said

"It's deeper. I woke up to a man named Jumbo and his wife Hagor. They told me they ran the Cuban Cartel and the American drug trade. He was Brazy and Rugar's plug who we never met or heard of," she said, confusing the room.

"Why the fuck are those Mexicans out there, son?" asked Bam Bam, looking out the windows.

"Chill, I'ma get there."

"What the fuck do Rugar got to do with you being kid-napped?" Big Smokey yelled, thinking she was lying.

"Everything, Blood." A male figure appeared in the shadows.

"What the fuck?" Big Smokey said as if he had seen a ghost.

"I knew you wasn't dead! It didn't add up," Bam Bam yelled as if he was in a movie when he saw Rugar come out in an all-red Tom Ford suit.

"Y'all need to tell us what's going on," Bullet said.

"As my wife was saying…" Rugar said as PYT smiled and showed her huge diamond.

"Damn, congratulations," everybody said, still upset at them.

"To sum this shit up, Blood, my uncle was the head of a cartel family and him and his wife left it to us," Rugar said. "I was in a coma. The doctors saved my life and I woke up to a new position. I met with all the powerful cartel families and now, since I'm running the Cuban Cartel, PYT is going to run the USA and the Empire while I play in the shadows. We have more power, money, and drugs then you can ever imagine," Rugar said.

Everybody was silent. They couldn't believe they were now dealing with the cartels.

"Damn, Blood I ain't know you was Cuban. You black as shit," Bullet said, making the room laugh.

"So what now?" Red Hat said.

"Where are you copping from?" Rugar asked.

"A cat in Miami named Ronell. He got the best shit in the States right now," Bam Bam said.

"Well, I'm back with the best work and price. How much y'all paying?"

"Nineteen," Bam Bam replied.

"I'ma give it to the Empire for fourteen apiece," Rugar said.

"Beef up security, get lawyers on retainers. Let's orchestrate our power," Rugar said.

"I saw your dead body at the morgue, Blood," Bam Bam said.

"I know, Blood. I was being watched for them bodies. But I'm good now. I'm connected," Rugar said.

"Look, I've been having a little issue. Somebody been hitting my spots and killing my men, but leaving drugs and money," Red Hat said.

"Damn. I'm going through the same shit, Blood. I lost a gang of men," Bam Bam said as Big Smokey said niggas did the same to one of his traps.

"I feel a war is on the rise," Red Hat said.

"Let's beef up security and focus on money. Has anybody spoken to Naya lately?" PYT said.

"We send her money every month," Bam Bam said.

"Glad to be back, but this is a new chapter," Rugar said, leaving while PYT finished the meeting.

Chapter 10
Newark, NJ

Muhammad sat Indian-style on the prayer rug in the mosque, reading from his noble Quran out loud to the sixty-something Muslims listening. The mosque was built from the ground up thanks to Muhammad and his crew last year.

It was a 24/7 mosque with a 24/7 security team guarding the mosque with their lives. Muhammad had robbed and killed one of the twins for his drugs. He'd been on major crews in major cities across the tri-state area thanks to his connect. He and his crew took over New Jersey and now they were focused on New York. Since Naya had left, New Jersey was a free-for-all. Muhammad's goal was to rob the rich and give to the poor, including selling poison. He used to have an African connect until he cut him off for whatever reason.

Lately, Muhammad had been sending crews to New York to take over turfs - all the Empire turfs. He had a plan to wipe out all gangbangers. He understood with no muscle there could be no army, so he was hitting their spots and killing their men.

Life was good for the brother. He had a large mansion in New Jersey with his first wife and eight kids. He had two more wives who lived in a different part of the mansion. He treated all of them equally.

"Father, why wasn't you at the night prayer?" Muhammad's son asked. He was the oldest of the eight at nineteen years old and had born in D.C. along with three of his brothers. Their father moved them all to New Jersey so they could help control his Empire. Young Malik was well-trained to kill. He was Muhammad's personal hit man

"Salaam-alaikum. I was in BK. I had to clean some shit up. But I want you to continue the good work. Where are your brothers?" Muhammad asked, looking up from his Quran in his office.

"Haleem is in B-More, Hasse is in Harlem with the other ocks up there, and Jalee is in Boston handling the financial affairs," Young Malik stated with his handsome baby face.

"I need you to be more Waiali (responsible) when you put in work. Stop getting messy," Muhammad stated.

"Sorry, but that wasn't me. I just send them in. But I got it, Pops."

"Good. The New York mission won't be so easy," Muhammad said as he nodded and left. He had to attend to a mission in a few hours.

***

Brooklyn, NY

Bam Bam was in Bubble's crib getting his dick sucked. She was going crazy on the dick, bobbing up and down on it, deep throating his shaft as cum filled her throat.

"Ummmm, daddy," she moaned, sucking every drop, making loud slurping noises while he laid back on her air mattress, looking at the ceiling in the empty room. There was no TV, but her head game was so good he thought he might have to pay for a flat screen.

Bubbles got off her knees, ready to fuck. She had been sucking dick for an hour and her jaws were hurting. She wanted to cum. But his fat little dick was limp. It was blowing her shit. Bubbles was thirty-five and beautiful with a reddish weave, light skin, tats, piercings, and a phat ass with stretch marks. Her pussy was phat with a Brazilian wax and it was extra wet, but from the three kids, her pussy wasn't as tight as it used to be.

Bam Bam looked in her face and could tell she wanted to fuck, but then his phone went off and he saw that it was an emergency text from his crew in Brownsville. He started to get dressed as her face turned red.

"That's fucked up," she said when she saw him getting dressed.

Bam Bam grabbed her by her weave and tossed her into the wall, about to stomp her out

"Bitch, you better be at work on time tomorrow," Bam Bam said, tossing her three hundred dollars.

She looked at him with tears as he walked out. Bubbles was a dancer at his hole in the wall strip club.

***

Bam Bam always had two trucks fill of goons surrounding him at all times. He pulled up to the Brownville Projects to see the block was hot with caution tape.

"What happened?" Bam Bam asked when Manta came to the truck window to talk to his boss.

"Blood, we was all bagging up shit and then we heard gunshots out here, so we ran outside and it was World War 3. Blood, it was ten of them with assault rifles. Kids, homies, old people was all dying, bro," Manta said as police continued to search the hood for clues.

"I'm out, bro. Nigga is playing a dangerous game."

"Oh shit, I forgot to tell you. They all had on Muslim garments. Bro, we went toe to toe with them. I'ma bounce out of town for the night," Manta said, walking through the lot as Bam Bam pulled off in deep thought.

Romell Tukes

Chapter 11
Port Chester, NY

PYT stood in the new mansion she had just purchased, looking at the freshly-painted ceiling and the marble floors shining like a mirror.

Rugar had flown out to Miami to take care of some personal business, then he would fly back to Cuba. He just got a message from one of Jumbo's doctors saying he would soon be placed on a deathbed because his cancer was spreading through his liagments.

The neighborhood was lovely, filled with rich lawyers, rappers, and judges from all over Westchester. It was a perfect area for her with lots of security. With sixteen acres of land, she was free to do as she pleased. There was a five bedroom guest house, five bedrooms in the main house, three bathrooms, a six car garage, a large pool in the back, a large basement she made into a gym, a bar, a pool room, and a large driveway the length of a football field.

"Aunty, my room has a waterbed," lil Brandon said as he ran downstairs with the nanny behind him.

"I know you would like it, baby. Did you see your game room down the hall?" she asked as his eyes widened.

"Are you serious?" he asked, running down the hall.

"After that, it's bath time. That boy is so happy you're back. He was driving me crazy asking about his aunty and uncle every day in Albany," the nanny said as the two walked into the large wall-to-wall carpeted living room.

"Yeah, I know, he getting so big," PYT said, watching the security team set up the guesthouse on the side of the house where they will be living.

Monica, the nanny, knew something of the lifestyle Rugar and PYT lived. She was okay with it, but she just wanted them to spend more time with Brandon because he had love for them. She had no idea Rugar had been shot. He told her they were on a serious vacation, but everything was cool now. Rugar spent time with Brandon before he went back to Miami.

"All those men surrounding the house are licensed to carry guns on the hip, right?" the nanny asked, knowing it looked like a mob boss lived here instead of a family.

"Yes, they're all licensed and trained to kill. Four of them will be with you at all times to protect you and Brandon. Me and my husband are connected to some powerful people now, so our family's safety is first," PYT stated, fixing her off-white dress.

"Okay. I'm about to cook dinner. Are you in the mood for anything special?" Monica asked.

"We have a maid for that, Monica," said PYT, following her into the kitchen.

"I sent her home, love," she replied, pulling out pots and pans, ready to cook up some soul food.

"Now that you're back, what are you going to do? Whatever happened to that business you were trying to open?" the nanny asked, chopping up onions and green peppers.

"I have two companies in Manhattan that are doing very well. I have a big meeting to expand my multi-million dollar company," she said, sitting on a stool and eating a plum as Monica nodded her head.

Before she was kidnapped, she had opened two companies on Wall Street with the help of the Empire. She was the face behind the company. She let the Jews run the daily operations because she knew it would have been hard to deal with investors. A successful and well-educated black woman would destroy most men's egos.

"Good luck," Monica said while tossing oil in the pans.

The women talked and both helped prepare dinner for themselves, Lil Brazy, and the twelve guards.

***

Miami, FL

It was 95 degrees out and the sun was beaming down. This was a normal day in the city.

"Did you see that little fat kid who would have drowned if it wasn't for that lifeguard? Who would let their children go out that far?" China said to Pressure, walking with him towards her apartment. They were both wearing summer gear. China wore sandals, showing her pretty manicured feet, and a bikini under her favorite sundress. Her hair hung to her lower back, dripping water.

"Yeah, too bad I can't swim. But I bet his fat ass knows better than to go in that deep water again," he said, laughing. His diamond grill shone like a light as it reflected off the sun. Pressure heard cars moving slow behind him as if someone was creeping when they were twenty-five feet away from China's building.

A second later, two all-black trucks pulled up, followed by a black and white 625 Maybach with tinted windows. Pressure continue to walk with China as she talked about plans for later. He pulled out two Glock 45 pistols when he saw a gang of Spanish niggas hop out in army gear.

The Latin men pulled weapons out after he did, but they had no clue they were up against the deadliest man in Florida. He stood in front of China fearlessly. Little did he know she had pulled out a .380 special and aimed it at the goons. She stood by his side, ready to shoot. He was shocked.

"What the fuck y'all want? Y'all got five seconds," Pressure said seriously.

The back door to the Maybach slowly opened up and a man in an all-red Gucci suit stepped out.

"Oh my fucking God! It can't be!" China screamed. Her gun fell and tears poured from her eyes as she ran to Rugar.

The two embraced tightly. China touched his face, shoulder, and neck to make sure it was really him, and it was. Pressure and Rugar's goons were still at gunpoint while Pressure tried to figure out what the fuck was going on.

"Put your guns down," Rugar told his men softly.

One of them said something in Spanish and they lowered their weapons as Pressure did the same, but still clutched it in his hand.

"I thought you was fucking dead! I can't believe this shit!" she said, wiping his tears.

"Almost, but our uncle saved me," he said, seeing how beautiful she had gotten in less than two years.

"Uncle? What are you talking about?" she asked, confused.

"It's a long story. Can I explain it over dinner?" he said while he and Pressure made eye contact.

"Sure. Oh, come meet my boyfriend that I love," she said, giving him a serious look so he would be nice.

Pressure was standing his ground, ice grilling the Spanish niggas, when Rugar pulled up

"Babe, this is Rugar, my brother that I told you about," she said.

He looked at her as if she was crazy because she had told him Rugar was dead.

"Nice to meet you," Rugar said, extending his hand as the two shook hands firmly.

"Likewise," Pressure said. He had heard a lot about him before he started dealing with China because he had family up top.

"I read your résumé, Pressure. Respect, bro. But I like how y'all was looking like Bonnie and Clyde a minute ago. I see you're willing to protect my sister with your life. That's all I need to see to give you my approval. Next time, don't hesitate," Rugar said, laughing.

"Normally I wouldn't, but I didn't want to put her life in the crossfire," he replied honestly.

"Facts. But I gotta fly back to Cuba later, so let's go eat. Bring Pressure along," Rugar said, walking back to the Maybach.

"Cuba? What the fuck? Come on, babe," she told Pressure.

"Nah, babe, go with your brother out to dinner. I'll see you later, okay?" he said, passing her the pistol she had dropped.

"Okay, love you," she said, kissing him and running off into the Maybach as the trucks full of goons pulled off.

Pressure was shocked that Rugar was alive. He had heard so much about Rugar. Even when he was doing time in the feds, his niggas from New York would always talk about the king of the city up top.

Chapter 12
Wall Street

PYT - or as her firm called her, Jasmine - walked into the skyrise glass building with two guards trialing her. She walked past crowds of businessmen and women entering and exiting the building.

"Excuse me, I'm here to speak to CEO Mr. Kraitzman and COO Mr. Zoeman," PYT said. She was in a suit and blazer looking very professional and wearing glasses as she approached the lobby clerk.

The clerk was a skinny middle-aged white woman who had recently started months ago and she already hated her job.

"May I ask your name? And are these men here to see them too?" she asked, hoping the two large men were there to fuck her boss up because he deserved it.

"My security will remain downstairs while I have my meeting with my workers, but I'm Ms. Jasmine Brown," said PYT as the clerk's eyes bulged open.

"Oh shit, I'm so sorry, Ms. Jasmine. I see your name on all of my checks. They're on the 19th floor. Do you need an escort?" she asked, feeling embarrassed and a little nervous.

"No, I'm good. Keep up the good work. I'ma make sure you get a bonus next check, Ms. Cyrus," said PYT while walking off in her red bottoms heels. Her two guards posted downstairs. PYT loved the stucco and ballast stone surrounding the unique lobby.

**

Upstairs in a large conference room, a group of businessmen and women tried to put their brains together to become more successful.

"I believe we need to expand more overseas. We have so many companies that are willing to let us profit off their brand overseas, so why not?" Mr. Kraitzman stated. He was rich and bloodthirsty. He had started off as a lawyer and now was one of the biggest accountants in the USA.

"How do you propose we come up with all this money?" a young pretty woman asked. She was sitting in the back writing in a notebook.

Before he answered, PYT walked in and posted up at the head of the table. "That's where I come in at, Ms. Patricia. Good morning, everybody. I'm sure I'm not late," she said, looking everyone in their eyes.

"Good to have you here, boss. Now we can begin," Mr. Zoeman said.

Everybody talked, brainstormed together, and came up with ideas and agreements.

After the long presentations, everybody came up with ideas to expand the company to other countries.

***

Queens, NY

Bam Bam and Red Hat were popping bottles in a club Bullet owned called Mercy. It was a gentlemen's club, so dancers were running around shaking asses and popping pussies on the stage, in VIP, on the floor, and in front of whoever had dollars.

"Damn, homie, this shit is popping, Blood. This nigga got disco lights. This ain't the 70's," Red Hat said, watching his goons go crazy tossing money everywhere as if they owned the place.

The stage was positioned in the middle of bar, but it was hard to receive tips back there or pay the bartenders because the dancers were getting all the money and stealing their shine. Men would rather look at a bitch popping pussy then a cute bitch trying to serve a drink.

"Facts. This is litty. But check this shit out. I got wind that some Muslims in Harlem are selling major work and they drilling it. I found some little ock nigga and told him to set up a meeting with their leader," Bam Bam said, looking at two Brooklyn niggas about to fight over a bitch

"And?" Red Hat asked.

"He want to meet at a factory in S.I. At first I was going to have the homies air that shit, but I don't know, Blood, I want to hear this shit," he said.

"Fuck them. They kill ten of ours, we kill sixty of theirs. I'm irritated, but I'ma leave it to PYT. She been waiting for this, so let her handle it. Plus she the boss now," Red Hat said as they drank and partied for the rest of the night.

***

Staten Island, NY

Muhammad sat in his little factory. It was located behind a train station. Security surrounded the factory like it was Fort Knox

"They're late, ahkee," Young Malik said, standing behind his pops, checking his G-Shock watch.

There was a loud whistle, letting them know their guests had arrived. There were at least eighty armed Muslims in the area.

Three large party busses arrived and three luxury cars all in red pulled up behind it. Bloods hopped out in all red with assault rifles. There were sixty or seventy of them now surrounding the building. It looked like a standoff outside.

Bam Bam, Bullet, and Red Hat walked into the factory with five men behind them. Malik laughed, showing his dislike for gang members.

"This is it. Who is the shot caller? One of you got to be the brains behind the legendary Empire," Muhammad said with a smirk.

"Curiosity killed the naked cat," a female voice said.

The Empire members moved to the side so PYT could walk through. When Muhammad saw her, he thought of Naya, because whoever she was, she looked just like her. PYT wore a red YSL dress and heels. She looked beautiful, showing her perfect frame and little breasts.

Muhammad thought it was a joke when he saw Bam Bam pull out the chair for her. But Young Malik tried not to stare. She was

59

the most beautiful woman he had ever seen in his life. His dick was hard.

"I don't know what type of games you playing, but I'm here to speak to y'all, not a hooker," Muhammad said with anger.

"Let's watch your fucking tone before you lose it," PYT stated seriously, making him get the picture.

"Who are you and where is the Rugar kid?" he now asked calmly. He had heard his name many times, not knowing he had gotten shot.

"I'm PYT. I run the Empire now. I didn't come here to waste time. You been sending your men to kill my army, so I'm here to get to the bottom line. So now my question is, who the fuck are you?" she asked while crossing her sexy legs.

"Okay, boss lady. I'm the one who's been causing mayhem. For one, I don't like gangbangers. For two, you have all the turf I want and need to move my product in," Muhammad said.

"Mr. Jones, I predict you ain't do 100% of your research on us."

"It's Muhammad," he corrected her.

"Whatever. But territories are not an option because the Empire and the Cartel eat in this land. So you can sell your dreams to New Jersey or Delaware. Now you can open a mosque on our turf, but there will be no drug selling, sex trafficking, or crimes in the area. You see, I'm a very fair lady. I have the Empire and a Cartel to run, so I can bend the rules," she said, making eye contact without a blink

"Cartel, huh? Look, I don't give a damn if it was the fucking Mafia. If I want something, I'ma take it. I won't let no bi——" He paused. "Nobody will tell me how to move!" Muhammad yelled.

"I'm sure we all have a rep to uphold. But I won't tolerate demands from a man who already drew blood on my land. So need I say more?" she said.

"I just wanted to get your attention."

"It's other ways to get people's attention, like phone calls, but your request for my turf is obviously vindictive, so I'ma forget we even had this conversation," PYT said. She stood up while patting her dress down, showing her classy side.

"Where do we go from here?" Muhammad asked.

"Well, you're a smart man. You believe in protocol and honor. Isn't that right, Young Malik?" PYT asked, staring at the handsome young man. He was shocked that she knew his name and even acknowledged him.

"Have a good evening, gentlemen," she said as she walked away. She stopped at the exit. "Muhammad, I hope you love flowers, because you will be seeing a lot of them," she said, getting him pissed as she walked out smiling, ready for war.

Chapter 13
Africa, years ago

"Zeema, tonight will test your fate," her father said as he led his young daughter into an underground dark cold tunnel where his tribe would hold slaves or rival tribal warriors.

Za'alya walked behind them both, smirking, wondering what her father had planned for PYT. But whatever it was, she knew it was dangerous.

"Daddy, I'm starving and weak," Zeema said while walking barefoot on dirt and rocks, hoping her father would be somewhat sympathetic to her.

Her father stopped and grabbed her small frail shoulders roughly. "This is your life. You're an assassin, not a kid. When it's time for you and Za'alya to take over my legacy, you will have to be prepared. The more you kill, the more power you will obtain," her father said, looking her in her gray eyes.

"Okay, Father," PYT replied, ice grilling her sister as they walked through the long narrow tunnel until they made it to a large dimly-lit room with a big cage.

The cage had two African men sitting on the floor with only cloth wrapped around their lower torsos, waiting on their fate, which was now standing in front of him. There were a couple of African men guarding the cage, waiting on their leader.

"Zeema, those two men in there are from another tribe. Kill them before they kill you," her father stated in their language. Normally they would speak Ndebele, but most of the rival tribes spoke Ndebele, Chewa, Nambya, Koison, Xhosa, Venda, or Chibarwa.

The guards passed all three of them swords, but it just so happened Zeema's sword was bigger and sharper. The men grabbed their swords and looked at each other, praying for freedom, knowing whoever they went against wouldn't be easy.

"Daddy, I want to kill the men, please," Za'alya said in a cry-baby voice, sounding jealous of her half-sister.

"Don't worry; I have a special mission for you tomorrow," he said, making her smile.

As Zeema walked towards the cage, the men looked at her as if she was a piece of meat. The men standing outside the cage unlocked it and pushed her inside.

"Fight for your freedom," her father told the men in their language as Za'alya laughed.

The men wasted no time. One of them rushed her at full speed. Both men was tall, chiseled, and ugly.

Zeema doubled back four steps while the man swung his sword wildly. She was able to side step, giving her an advantage. She stabbed him in his rib cage, making him stumble back holding his side in pain as blood squirted everywhere.

The other African attached PYT, barely missing her head as he tried to take it off. Luckily, she dodged it. She began swinging her sword like a ninja and backed him into the corner as their swords connected with every hard swing. The other attacker sneaked behind her, holding his side, and lunged at her with the sword in his good hand. Thanks to the look on the African's face, she knew someone was behind her. PYT dropped low to the floor in a split while the sword landed in the other African's heart killing him.

Before he was even able to pull out the sword out of his brother-in-law, a sharp pain shot through his spine, then his neck was sliced open. His body dropped in his brother-in-law's blood puddle.

The guards opened the gate for PYT. They were always impressed with her skills. She was the best they had ever seen besides her sister and aunt.

"Those two men were skilled sword fighters from the Chinhayl tribe. We sent twenty men in that cage, and none made it out alive," her father said sternly.

"Daddy, I could have did better, and they almost killed her," Za'alya stated, mad.

"Come on. We have a meeting," he said, walking off in his African gown.

"I swear, one day I'ma kill you," Za'alya said, pushing PYT onto the ground with force.

PYT got up and vowed to kill her sister before she got a chance to kill her.

***

PYT woke up from her deep dream sweating. She looked around her room as if someone was there. She climbed out of bed in her bra and panties and wrapped herself up in a robe as she walked to Lil Brazy's room to check on him.

She hated when she dreamed of the mother land, her sister, or her father. She hated even thinking about Africa. She felt as if she lost her soul out there.

After seeing Lil Brazy snore, she went to get dressed in her Under Armour gear for a late night workout. She walked past the security booth to see that they were on point.

Once in her private gym with its padded mats, a boxing ring, weights, pull-up bars, jump ropes, swords, rubber dummies, and exercise machines, she opened a glass case on the wall full of swords. She picked her favorite sword, which she had made in Seoul, South Korea.

She started with double flips while swinging the sword in the air as if she was sparring. She was doing roundhouse kicks at the speed of lightning as she went hard dancing with the sword for two hours.

***

Soundview, Bronx

Red Hat sat in front of the build with a crew of gangbangers with his little homie Twerk.

"When Murda coming back up top, son? He owe me a new Draco. He kidnapped my shit, Blood," Twerk said while smoking a Dutch cigar full of sour diesel, watching all the kids running around enjoying the day.

"He in Atlanta with Glizzy and P," Red Hat said, loving his hood in Soundview. He was the mayor, but Pistol Pete would always be the president, of course.

Red Hat had almost every hood in the BX under his authority, thanks to PYT. He was proud of her marriage and position with the Empire and Cartel. This was deep, but she deserved it. She had come a long way.

The other day she gave the green light to crush the Muslims on sight, but she knew the Muslims were deep. It would be a hard, tough war, but she was prepared.

"Yo, Hat. Melly from Courtland said niggas had a shootout with some ocks on the block!" A young kid ran up to them from out of the building yelling as everybody went to strap up.

"Game on," Red Hat told his crew as they all hopped in Hondas, Chevys, and Camaros.

When they arrived, the projects were flooded with NYPD and FBI. Yellow caution tape was hanging all over the place.

They whole hood was out crying at the craziest shooting they ever saw. It was like a 9/11 attack in the hood, leaving sixteen people dead.

"RJ, what happened?" Red Hat asked on the corner.

His goons watched the crying families watch the EMS trucks drive away with their loved ones.

"Yooo, son, it was like two hundred rounds going off. The homies all shot back, but them niggas with the big beards dressed in them long robes had some high power shit, brotty. They killed Pac, Taff, Joe, Low J, Beer, Snake, JJ, Randal, Number 9, and Ricky. Over sixteen niggas, bro," RJ stated, shaking his little head.

"Look, call a meeting at the spot in three hours," Red Hat said, walking off with his team behind him.

The Muslims had violated his most profitable hood. He had to show the wannabe desert monkeys who he was and what this Blood shit was about.

Chapter 14
Harlem, NY

Young Malik and his right hand man Bloody Ock sat behind the wheels of an all-black Chevy Equinox with tints. They were watching people walk up and down Lenox without a care in the world as the sun went down.

"That was good work, ock. I'm sure Muhammad is pleased. Those head wraps and sunglasses was good. I know we still on the world news," Malik said with a laugh.

"They labeled it a terrorist attack. When people make dangerous allegations like that, I feel as if they're only manipulating the media of the lost souls," Bloody Ock said on his Malcom X shit.

"Elaborate, nigga," Malik said.

"I'll save my theory for another time, ock. Inshallah. I'ma go check on our meal," Bloody Ock said, getting out of the car to walk into the halal spot.

Bloody Ock was from the east side of Harlem, a place called the border. Before he turned Muslim upstate, he used to be a big homie Blood gang member until his homies snitched on him. Bloody Billy used to be his name until he caught a ten year bid, thanks to a crew of Bloods snitching on him to get him off the streets because he was killing shit. He spent time in Attica and Sing-Sing, learning the Islamic deen, and he became very knowledgeable.

Once he came home, he practiced martial arts, finished college, studied other languages, and became a big figure in his community. After he picked up the halal food he and Malik had ordered, he talked to the Arabian store owners, who owned a chain of halal stores throughout Harlem.

The two drove to a secret location across town on St. Nick to chill with some brothers, then the two had to go out of town.

***

The brown stone apartment was full of Muslims. There were nine of them chilling, playing Xbox, reading the Quran, praying, studying, using drugs, and some were asleep.

"As-salaam-alaikum," Malik said to some Muslim brothers sitting on the couch near him.

"Walaikum salaam. You see we still on the news, ahkee. I lived in the Bronx twenty-nine years and I ain't never see no gangsta shit like that," Wali'a said as other Muslims there agreed.

Everybody in the room was against killing kids and women, but today was an honest mistake when two kids and two mothers got caught in the crossfire.

"Y'all want some?" Malik said, offering his ocks some of his food.

"No, we all already ate, but I believe Raheem ordered some pizza as well. But they late," Jabile said, checking his watch.

"Hassem is coming back and he got some shit lined up in Queens for us," Malik said.

The doorbell rang twice, snapping them out of whatever they were doing because they were ready to eat.

"I got it!" Umar ibn Haqq yelled. He was the youngest of the crew from Philly. As soon as Umar ibn Haqq opened the door, a bullet slammed into his skull.

Everybody went for cover and grabbed their weapons. They were prepared for this type of shit.

Twerk was the third nigga into the apartment as bullets came from everywhere. Gunmen came from under the table shooting and also from behind the kitchen counter.

"Damn, lift the couch!" Malik yelled as he fired rounds from his 9mm towards the ten niggas he just saw run inside the crib.

There were two loaded shotguns under the couch. Wali'a took one and passed one to Malik as bullets shot the stuffing out of the sofa.

"Don't hide now!" Red Hat yelled with a Draco in his hand, airing shit out, killing ocks back to back.

Three Muslims came out of one of the back rooms, letting off rounds from AK-47s, hitting four Bloods in their upper torsos while the rest of them took off, hiding and re-loading.

Red Hat saw Malik pop up from under a table while Twerk was creeping his way, unaware danger was there.

"Twerk!" yelled Red Hat

Boom! Boom! Boom!

Twerk's body ripped in half. Red Hat sent bullets his way, but he ducked and hid behind a wall. Wali'a tried to do the same, but he was shot in the face four times thanks to Red Hat.

Bloody Ock came out of a closet, shooting two Bloods in the back who were slipping. He had two Colt 45's in his hands, laughing. Malik and Bloody Ock were the only two Muslims left and there were four Bloods left

"We gotta go!" he yelled to Malik, who was only six feet away behind a wall.

Bloc! Bloc! Bloc! Bloc! Bloc!

The two ran towards the bathroom, trying to hold off Red Hat with bullets as he ducked and fired back. Bullets were weaving past them as they made it to the bathroom and climbed out the window, rushing down the fire escape.

"Fuck, I'm shot!" Bloody Ock yelled as he saw blood leaking down his arm. He landed on the floor while bullets sparked the ground from upstairs.

"Come on, ock, you tryna die?" Malik said, pulling him as they rushed down an alley.

***

Atlanta, GA

"This shit brazy, Blood," Murder said to Glizzy. He had just gotten off the phone with one of his homies, who informed him that Twerk had gotten killed last night.

"What happened, homie?" Glizzy asked as he whipped his dark red Donk on thirty inch rims through the College Park projects.

"Niggas is up top beefing with Muslims. Shit getting brazy, Blood," Murder said as he lit a blunt.

"Yeah, I saw that shit on the news. I thought it was a terrorist attack," Glizzy said, parking.

"I'ma head back home in a couple of days," Murder stated, walking through the hood now as if he owned it, dressed in a Givenchy outfit with shoes to match.

Lately, Murder had been down south networking in N.C., S.C, Alabama, N.O., and Kentucky with the help of Glizzy, who was now a kingpin.

Murder had a sexy redbone in the hood who worked at Magic City. Her head game was the best and the pussy was tighter than virgin pussy. She was a rider and she was a good girl dancing to pay for college and her bills.

Cherry had met Glizzy years ago. They were cool. He never even asked her for a dance, but she knew he was the king of the city. When she saw Murder with him in the club with his New York swag blowing a bag, he caught her eyes. That night, Murder dropped $15,000 on her, then took her out to eat. And the rest was history.

She was five feet tall, 141 pounds, thick, with C-cups, thick lips, and hazel eyes. She was high yellow with soft curly dark long hair and she had a couple of tattoos.

As soon as he walked in the crib, she had her legs wide open, moaning and fingering her pussy, ass naked. Thick cum was pouring on the leather couch as she fingered herself faster until she squirted across the room. Then she grabbed his dick, pulled it out of his jeans, and gave him a mean blowjob until she swallowed his kids.

Chapter 15
Florida woman's federal penitentiary

Naya came out of her Muslim afternoon prayer in a line with ten other women dressed in uniforms with hijabs covering their faces. The women in the unit prayed five times a day in the small activity room, where they would hold religious service daily.

Since Naya's sentence, she did everything in her power to remain humble, positive, and alive, even turning to Islam for comfort. Her deen kept her alive along with her appeal on her four life sentences, but she knew it was all the creed of Allah.

"That was good, Naya. Your Arabic is amazing. I love when you lead the prayer," Cat said in her soft sweet voice.

Cat was born a Muslim woman. She was Moroccan from a small tone town called Agadir. She was very beautiful: high yellow, bright green eyes, perfect smile, toned body, smooth skin, long, silky, jet black hair. When she was twenty years old and living in Austin, Texas, she was in college when she was raped by a dude she was dating. One day he tried to break into her dorm room on campus and rape her again, but she shot him sixteen times, killing him. When she started trial, there was no evidence of her being raped. She had never reported it because she was scared. Cat ended up blowing trial and was sentenced to life in prison. She was now twenty-five and she had lost all of her appeals already.

Everybody left the room as Naya and Cat walked out to the computer so they could email their loved ones. Naya heard the C.O. calling her for a visit with a slight attitude.

"I'ma go get ready. I'll see you when I get back," Naya told Cat as she waited in line for the computer.

Naya went into her small clean cell to see all types of books laying around - everything from *Life of a Savage* to *A Deadly Love Scam*, which was from her favorite author. She had a locker full of food and hygiene items and she had six large net bags full of snacks for her and her celly Cat.

Naya got dressed and freshened up, then she made her way out of the unit to see her best friend Ronell. She had not felt this way about a nigga since Brazy.

***

Ronell sat at the visit table, sipping out of a bottle of apple juice, waiting for the only woman who had his heart. Today he had a big surprise for her. He planned to marry her. He had already spoken to the prison officials and they had no issue with it.

He brought her a two million dollar wedding band because diamonds weren't allowed in the prison. Since he met her, his life had changed. She met him as a dancer and she never judged him. It had only been part time so he could get back on his feet since at the time, he was fresh home. He knew she was his soulmate. In jail or not, he wanted her. Yes, he still had his little side bitches he would fuck, but it was nothing more, and Naya was okay with it. He was a man.

Ronell looked around the empty visiting room, shaking his head because when women get locked up, niggas be leaving them for dead. Let a nigga get locked up, he'll be blowing a bitch's phone up crying, stressing, and losing his hair. He saw it all on his bid.

He saw Naya walking through the metal door in a gray sweat-suit with a pair of white Air Force Ones on her little feet. She was cute.

"Damn, you look nice today. Business meeting today?" she asked as she gave him a hug and kiss, looking at his all-black Tom Ford suit.

"Something like that. But how you holding up, beautiful?" he said, holding her soft hands

"I talked to the appeals lawyer. We still waiting for a response. Besides that, I'm in my prayers, Quran, and exercises 1-2 hours a day with the girls. I got to put you on to this Ubron novel called *A Gangsta Quran 1-4*. OMG, shit is popping," Naya said, excited.

"I'ma check into it. But how you getting along with the bad girl club in there?" he asked, looking into her exotic eyes.

"They okay. A chick came in last week. She got caught trafficking twenty-one keys for her boyfriend and took ten years. She was telling everybody about a nigga in Miami who had the city on lock and when bitches was asking for the nigga's name, she said she didn't know. But she told us he was sexy as hell and owned a club. I wanted to stab this bitch. She so dumb. But just move a little lighter," Naya said, looking around to see bitches eyeing her man. She didn't mind as long as they stayed in their place.

"I got you, boo. But fuck that jailhouse gossip. You know how people talk. On another note, love, Pressure told me yesterday that China's brother came back in town on some pop up from the dead shit," Ronell stated.

Naya's face held a crazy look. "What? Who? Are you sure? It can't be."

"Rugar. A young kid," he said, not really knowing too much about him or their history aside from what Pressure told him.

"I can't believe this shit! I thought he was dead," she said, confused.

"Pressure said dude hopped out with two trucks full of Spanish guards as if he was down with the Mafia or some shit. I heard his Maybach wasn't even out in the States yet. Pressure met him, said he was cool, and he let the two of the build. He said he never saw China so happy," said Ronell.

"Damn. I can't believe this shit."

"Did you get the phone?" he asked in a low voice. He had guards on his payroll in there so she could get whatever she wanted: iPhones, tablets, drugs, weapons, designer clothes, and takeout food, whatever she desired.

"Yeah, I got it this morning, but I hate dealing with the police. They real funny style," she said.

"I got a big surprise for you today, baby," he said, pulling out a wedding band and standing up before getting down on his knee. "Will you marry me?" he asked her.

"Yesss!" she said, grabbing his face and kissing him.

"Good," Ronell said. He called one of the guards over to him so he could get the marriage papers so she could sign it. As soon as she signed it, the chapel was already set up waiting for them as two prison guards escorted them over there.

Once they got married, the shit felt so different. It was something both of them wanted.

***

Cuba

Rugar sat inside Jumbo's office, drinking a cup of mint tea, something he had recently started along with his exercising. Rugar just shipped over fifty tons of drugs to the cartel families. They were fucking with him heavy.

"You okay, young'un?" Jumbo asked as he pulled out a cigar and lit it as if he wasn't sick and barely able to walk. He used a cane or walker to get around. The doctors told him that he should be on bedrest but he refused, almost firing all of them.

"I'm straight. Just worrying about my wifey. She got a couple of issues back home," he replied, thinking about what PYT told him last night on Facetime about her going at it with the ocks.

"Trust me, kid, the men you have stationed with her are well-trained and war ready," Jumbo said, laughing.

"I understand. But she isn't trying to mix the Empire war with the Cartel affairs, plus she said they have more than enough soldiers to win a war with the Muslims," Rugar said, checking his Rolex watch

"Trust me, relax. PYT is good. She has wings over her that you know nothing about. She is well-protected at all times," Jumbo said, coughing.

"I believe you. But I'ma head back to the States on the private jet after I meet the Asian family. They want to talk about the nuclear war missiles we have but I believe they have some new shit that could be useful," Rugar said.

"Oh yes, be smart. They are very cunning, witty, and prideful people, and the governor wants to meet you here for dinner tonight," Jumbo said as he stood to leave.

"Okay, I'ma head across town in the city," Rugar said.

"Be careful," Jumbo said, knowing Cuba was known to kidnap for ransom, then kill whoever. And since Rugar was an out of town kid, he would be an easy target.

"I know. I got two bulletproof Hummers and a team with me at all times, plus I'm strapped. I'll never get caught slipping again," he said. He walked out of the office to see Savannah standing there in her training gear tights and a tight shirt.

"Hey there," she said in good English. Lately she had been studying the English language.

"What's up, Savannah? What you up to?" he asked, wondering why she was that close to the doors, as if she had been eavesdropping. He looked down to see the biggest camel toe he ever saw. When she saw this, she started to smile.

"I'm going to talk to Papa about more security and more weapons for the compound down the block," Savannah said, moving closer to him while looking down at his semi-hard penis poking out of his slacks.

Rugar could feel her breasts on his chest and her strong perfume smelled good. She was turning him on. He couldn't take it.

"I'll see you around," he said, racing off. Her hard nipples, phat pussy, and the freaky look she gave him had his dick jumping.

Savannah licked her lips as he rushed downstairs. She laughed as she turned around and went the other way, switching her little soft ass so that it jiggled with every step.

Chapter 16
Queens, NY

Bullet and Big Smokey were in a low-key Jamaican restaurant surrounded by goons.

"You own a lot of shit. You own this piece of shit too?" Big Smokey asked, being sarcastic while sucking the soft meat off the oxtails he was eating.

"Yes I do, Blood. Too bad you don't invest your money," Bullet stated with a chuckle as Big Smokey stopped eating and got serious.

"You don't know what the fuck I do with mines. I'll never let millions I put my blood, sweat, and tears into go to waste. I got three limo services in Las Vegas banking in millions yearly. What the fuck you talking about?" Big Smokey said with his deep voice.

"'Bout time, Blood, something legit," Bullet said, not believing a word he saying. Bullet was one of the most successful men in the Empire because he was a legit entrepreneur making a fortune from his own success. With seven businesses, he was ahead of his time. He had started off as a lookout kid for big time hustlers in Queens. Now he was seeing more millions than a bank teller.

"I ain't come to pocket check you, Blood. I called this meeting to enlighten you on a move we should make on the ock," Bullet said, getting his attention.

Since the war, Bullet and Big Smokey had teamed up to make Queens, Long Island, and Staten Island a stronger force and they did just that, even though they never saw eye to eye.

"Speak the block, Bill Gates. You got the floor," Big Smokey said, smirking, getting under Bullet's skin.

"Friday afternoon when the ocks come out of Jumah, we hit them all in front of the mosque. Muhammad and his crew always come out first. We been watching. I believe he owns the place. He rolls deep, but we roll deeper. Red Hat almost caught the young boy slipping, but he got loose. I heard that shit was fucking crazy. But what you think?" Big Smokey stated.

Bullet was silent for some seconds, thinking about the female Muslims and kids that could lose their lives. It was risky. Bullet's whole family was Muslim, so it made him feel funny, but it was war time.

"Shooting in a mosque or outside of one will bring the Feds and Homeland to our doorstep. But how far do they walk down the block?" Bullet asked.

"They park two blocks away in a big lot that belongs to the mosque in L.I., Blood, but it's a good distance away from the mosque," Big Smokey said, which he knew from all the times he parked there watching their daily activity.

"Okay, then we hit them there or a little further down the block," Bullet said as Big Smokey stood up in agreement.

"Hold on, big man. You think I'm paying for your meal? This not on the house. You ate three plates," Bullet said as Big Smokey pulled out a wad of twenties and tossed it on the table.

"Cheap-ass nigga!" Big Smokey yelled as he walked out with the ten man crew he rolled with.

***

Long Island, NY

Haleem and his crew had just come back from B-More, Maryland. They were on the west side of the city taking over blocks, warring with the city to come out on top.

Today was Friday Jumah and Imam Yusuf was taking Muhammad's spot in giving the service since Muhammad was giving the service in New Jersey at another mosque.

Iman Yusuf was sixty-five years old, healthy, with gray hair. He was very intelligent, genuine, and he loved the believers. He had built two mosques in Philly on the south side and north side where he was raised. Growing up in the city of Brotherly Love, he was a gun clapper known for busting his heat in his younger age.

The mosque was packed as he gave the Friday sermon, then led the brothers in prayer. Afterwards, Haleem approached the Iman, telling him how amazing the service was.

Haleem was Malik's twin, but darker and younger. He had just turned eighteen years old. He was from Northeast, D.C. He was a known killer in his city since the age of fifteen.

"Thanks for taking my pops' place," Haleem told him as he packed his briefcase with Islamic material.

"No need to thank me. It's a blessing from Allah. I'll see you around. As-salaam-alaikum," Iman Yusuf said as he left the mosque with the eight man crew he always traveled with for protection.

Haleem and his crew followed them outside, where everybody was leaving, talking, about to go back inside the mosque to make the afternoon prayer that was about to come on.

Haleem had to go to Harlem to talk to young Malik about this war he had been hearing about because he had been in B-More for months.

He saw Yusuf climb in a large van that could fit sixteen passengers. Haleem tailed them in two Tahoe trucks full of ocks trained to go.

"That was off the hook, Yusuf," said the driver of the large van that held Yusuf and his crew.

Before he could even reply, two large Chevrolet Silverados rammed into the van, flipping it over at high speed in an intersection with heavy traffic, but luckily, it was empty.

Six small vans pulled up with the doors open, full of goons with guns and red flags. Haleem wasted no time. He hopped out of his Tahoe with his goons, shooting at the niggas flooding the streets in red.

Shots were going back and forth in the middle of the streets. Haleem waited to check on Yusuf, who was being helped out of the flipped van by three of his men. Everyone else was dead either off of impact or the bullets the Bloods shot into the van.

Gunmen were everywhere. Niggas were being shot left and right, Yusuf had a pistol. In shooting back, he hit two of the Bloods in the head while Haleem caught a Blood from behind in the back of the head. Yusuf started to go crazy, yelling, shooting every nigga in sight while laughing

"Yusuf, look out!" Haleem yelled, ducking from bullets.

Two Bloods sneaked behind Yusuf and blew his brains on the pavement, then tried to take out the rest of them.

Bullet was now leaning on a parked car after killing the old man who was shooting wildly, but he was trying to touch the young nigga who took out six of his men alone.

Haleem was shooting at Big Smokey, who was bopping and weaving and dodging bullets while shooting back as guns barked from everywhere. He only saw three of his men left and there were at least eight of them left.

"Fuck!" Haleem yelled as he saw them closing in on him quickly. He took off running to the Tahoe until he felt pain shoot through his back and side. He dropped before he even got halfway because he was hit seven times.

Haleem turned on his back to shoot at the men running his way, but his 9mm clicked because he was out of bullets. Blood soaked his white garment. He saw a big black nigga block the sunlight as he stood over him with a pistol.

"Damn, Blood, you put up a fight, son," Big Smokey said as he heard sirens closing in on him.

"Allah Akbar, you big-ass nigga!" Haleem yelled before Big Smokey emptied his clip into his frail young body.

Big Smokey ran, getting in the van and pulling off.

Chapter 17
Bronx, NY

Murder walked inside Red Hat's barber shop located in the Highbridge section of the BX with Cherry behind him

"Yo, Murder, what's good, my guy?" Taz asked while cutting a little kid's hair.

"What's shaking, boy? I see y'all busy tonight," Murder said, walking through the packed shop.

Everybody looked at Cherry's ass and curves poking out of her Givenchy tight jeans and her beautiful facial features.

"Money Saturday. But who is that? They don't even build like that around here," Taz said, wondering what her measurements were.

"She off limits, son. Put your tongue back in your mouth, Where your boss at?" Murder said as he nodded his head towards the back room.

The two walked to the back as everybody started yelling and screaming, trying to compare her to other bitches with crazy asses.

Cherry was used to it since middle school and high school, and when she became a stripper in Atlanta, her name spread like wildfire. She was happy he let her come to New York to start a new life. At first it was only about his money, but now she was really feeling him. He had just bought her a condo, a Mercedes-Benz CLS450 sliver and gray spaceship, and he gave her 50K so she could open up her dream lingerie store. Now all she had to do was obtain her business license next week. She asked him why he was doing all of this and he told her he just wanted to see her happy. When he said that, they fucked all night unprotected, something she never did with any nigga.

In the private back room, Red Hat was on the phone as the two beautiful Spanish bitches counted money and placed it in big stacks.

"Y'all niggas need to handle that tonight," Red Hat said, hanging up upset. He looked at Murder, then looked at Cherry as if she was lost.

"Who the fuck is she?" Red Hat asked Murder, knowing she wasn't from around there.

"Hey, I'm Cherry," she said in a country voice, extending her hand.

Red Hat looked at her manicured nails as if blood was on them.

"She's with me," Murder said, knowing his friend could get disrespectful with women quick.

"Nigga, while you in Atlanta hunting for a piece of pussy, we losing homies every day. We just lost eleven last night in Webster and on Weeks Avenue," Red Hat said, drinking from a bottle of black Henny.

"I'ma excuse myself, baby. I'll be in the car," Cherry said, walking out.

The Spanish bitches stared at her wide ass, which could barely fit through the door.

Cherry had heard about murders and saw all the money in the room. There had to be over three million there. She now knew Murder was a part of some serious shit.

"You just met that bitch and got her ass done," Red Hat said, shaking his head.

"That's all hers, bro. But look, I got a plan. Excuse me for a minute, ladies," Murder told the two Spanish women.

They stood up looking like twins with lots of make-up and fake body parts.

"Okay, papi," they both said, smiling as they walked into the back room were niggas were shooting dice.

***

Newark, NY

Muhammad sat in his mosque Indian style, in deep thought, thinking about the killing of his son and Iman Yusuf. The phone ringing took him out of his thought process.

"As-salaam-alaikum," Muhammad said as he answered the phone in a raspy voice. The caller gave him an address to write down, which made him smile brightly.

Young Malik walked into his pops' quiet room to see him smiling, but it was about to be washed away.

"They killed Kathir last night with six other Muslims all dressed in their garments. Even the killers wore garments to trick them. This took place in the Bronx by Yankee Stadium I know it was Red Hat and his side kick pops. I'ma spread their blood like butter," Malik said, remembering his older cousin Kathir who was gifted in reciting the Quran.

"Don't worry. Allah is on our side. I just got PYT's home address and I have a plan," Muhammad said coldly.

**

Argentine, Cuba

Rugar was at his other mansion watching six trucks pull away from his driveway. He had just had a business meeting with the Santiago Cartel family from Guatemala. His personal maid was an older Spanish women who knew little English, but she helped him study Spanish on his free time.

She brought him a hot cup of tea and a pastry.

"Muchas gracias," he said.

She walked off to prepare dinner for later before the Colombia Cartel family was supposed to arrive tonight.

Rugar called PYT every day, but he missed her touch, sex, taste, and company. Everything was perfect when she was around. He got up from the living couch and went upstairs to take a shower then a nap. He had a long day and it was only 2 p.m.

Jumbo and Hagor were out of town on a date enjoying the little time he had left because it was getting bad. He had lost thirty pounds in two weeks.

Rugar walked into his master bedroom and closed the door to hear moans. The room curtains wear closed so the room was dark.

Rugar turned on the lights and pulled out a gun, but what he saw paused every bone in his body

Savannah was lying butt naked on his bed with a picture of him in her left hand while she used her right hand to play in her pussy.

"Ohhhh…mmm…ohhh…" she moaned, fingering her phat, clean-shaved pussy as she made loud noises from her pussy. "Ugggh, I'm about to…uhhh!" she moaned, going faster in her tight pussy, staring at Rugar's hard dick while she dropped his picture and sucked on her titty.

"Uhhhh, I'm cumming!" she screamed. "Papi, papi, ya vay! Ya vay!" she yelled as she squirted across the room on the floor.

Rugar felt his pre-cum drip down his legs. She got up and worked towards him. They were now face to face. She placed her finger in his nose so he could smell her flower scent.

"Please, papi, take my virginity. Make me a woman. I want to suck your dick and feel you in my tight walls," she said as she quickly got on her knees and grabbed his hard dick, surprised at how big it was.

"No, no, no, stop, put your clothes on. Get up," he said as she almost unbuckled his slacks. Even though she had turned eighteen years old three days ago, Rugar couldn't do it, even thought she had him on another level, horny as hell.

"Please, I swear I won't tell! Please, I want you and need you, papi!" she cried, still trying to grab his dick.

"Stop it, no more!" he said, grabbing her and tossing her on the wall as she was still trying to grab his dick to suck. "Go get dressed now before I hurt you," he said seriously as she ran to get dressed with tears in her eyes.

"Si yo fuera lo penseria dos veces (I'd think twice about that if I was you)," she said, fully dressed and looking at his still-hard dick before leaving pissed off.

"I'm married," he said while he slammed the door, sitting angrily on the soaked bed full of thick cum.

Chapter 18
Lower Eastside, NY

Agent Norris sat in his condo going over some old and new photos of gruesome murders that made his stomach flip. The more he thought about all the gang killings, the more shit started to come together. The city two years ago was the Wild Wild West: broad daylight shootings, kids and elderly women getting killed in the crossfire.

Morris couldn't figure out why Thomas and Wilson didn't crack the case before it got to the FBI. His boss told him to leave it alone or his job would be on the line. He understood all the stress and pressure that was put on his boss from Washington and the media.

Not only did his informants tell him something big was going on but he felt it, plus lately there had been a lot of dead Muslims and gang members popping up around the city. He kept hearing the name PYT, a woman that was now the ring leader of the Empire.

Morris did his research to come up with nothing on the PYT person. She was like a ghost. He was starting to think his snitches were all lying. One thing he knew for certain was the drug activity in the city was on the raise: 46% in the last ninety days.

"Who are you, PYT? I'm going to find you," he said, leaning back in his chair, thinking.

"What did you say, baby?" Patricia said, coming out of the room with a robe covering her petite frame as she walked towards him.

"I'm just trying to crack this case. It was a name I said. PYT is a person I'm trying to link to some of this mayhem. But anyway, how was your night, beautiful?" he asked.

She was sitting in his lap with an awkward look on her face as if she had seen a ghost.

Patricia was Puerto Rican. She was raised in the Bronx near Fordham Road in poverty with her mother. She was very beautiful, as if she could be a model. At twenty-six years old she was single with no kids and a senior rep at an account firm in the city. Four years ago she was homeless and living in a van, working at strip clubs all over the Bronx.

One night at work, she was taking a break at the bar where she met PYT and the two talked for over an hour. PYT was there to meet Red Hat, who owned the club, but when PYT met Patricia, she liked her vibe. She could tell she was a sweet girl. Pat told her she was dancing because she lost her parents and was now homeless.

When she told her she had to go back to work, PYT told her to take off. Pat refused, telling her that her boss Red Hat ran a tight shift. PYT gave her $900 and told her Red Hat was her brother, but Pat refused to take her money. She refused to sleep with customers or downgrade herself like the other women normally did when they worked.

Pat left that evening and came back the next day ready to twerk and dance to make a dollar. The club security got Pat from the dressing room and told her the boss wanted to see her while they escorted her upstairs.

Once in the upstairs office, PYT gave her a warm smile and friendly hug, then she told her today would be her last of dancing. Pat was pissed, trying to beg for her job, but PYT told her she had something else planned for her

"This isn't for you, Pat. Go to school, get your business and accountant degree with me. I'ma build a big firm and I want you to be a part of it. I will pay for your clothes, college, housing, food, and car. I just think you deserve better. I'm not doing this because I feel sad for you. I just see so much off myself in you," PYT told her.

Pat was speechless. "I'm not gay," was all Pat could say as PYT laughed so hard.

"Sorry, I'm strictly dickly," PYT said, laughing.

That was the start to their loyal friendship. PYT did everything she said she would, and now Pat was a big time accountant on Wall Street.

She met Morris six months ago and the two had been fucking since, but it was nothing more than a fuck. He knew nothing of Pat's background expect that she was a wealthy accountant.

Pat got up and went to use the bathroom as Morris finished his project. She locked the bathroom door and texted Red Hat's old number, asking for PYT's number because she had to meet with her ASAP.

***

Florida Federal Women's Prison

Naya walked into the visiting room looking healthy, bright, beautiful, and like her regular self.

PYT got up to hug her sister tightly, trying to hold back her tears.

"Oh my God, you look good and you getting thick on the jail-house food," PYT said as they both sat down.

"It's been so long. I was worried sick about you, Jasmine. I had no clue you was coming. I heard Rugar's alive? Where was you?" Naya asked, trying to figure this shit out because these questions had been on her mind for weeks.

"Hold up. You're fucking married?" PYT said, looking at her wedding band, shocked.

"Yeah, last month, to this guy named Ronell from Miami, I fell in love with him. Never in a million years would I think I'd fall in love again after Brazy," she said.

"That's crazy, because I got married to Rugar in Cuba," PYT said, flashing her diamond ring with a bright smile

"Damn, that shit is fucking huge! You two deserve it. I still can't believe he is alive. How?" Naya asked.

"I'll get to that in a second. But how's your appeal?" PYT asked.

"Waiting. My lawyers putting in motions," she stated.

"That's a blessing. Anyway, Rugar survived the shooting from Lil C, but I took care of him," she said, giving Naya a look she know too well. "That nigga…I thought he was dead. Everybody did. But I knew there was something wrong when I called every hospital to find him only to get nothing. I went to my condo and I was kidnapped. Girl, they shot me with some shit that put me out cold," she told Naya as she listened. "When I woke up, I was Cuba with Jumbo and his wife," PYT said.

"Hold on, Brazy's old connect?" Naya said, shocked.

"Yeah, listen, damn. So I wake up and they tell me Rugar's in a coma and they run the Cartel organization or some crazy shit. When Rugar wakes up, I tell him that Jumbo is his uncle and wants us both to take over the Cuba Cartel because he is his only bloodline and Jumbo's sick. I run the U.S. and 85% of the drug trade is from us. I also run the Empire while Rugar is in Cuba," PYT said in her low-pitched voice.

"Wow, that's crazy! This another level. But you sure you can handle this and the Empire?" Naya asked seriously.

"Of course! But we having issues with a Muslim nigga named Muhammad. It's a big war right now," she replied.

"Muhammad from Newark?" Naya asked, wondering if it was her old customer and longtime friend.

"I have no clue. But my patience is running very thin. Do you know him?" PYT asked.

"Hell yeah! I'm the one who showed him the game. But he crossed me by killing one of the twins. I thought he was dead or on the west coast somewhere. I can't believe he got the balls to fuck with the Empire," Naya stated, pissed.

"He got a big team of Muslims on his side and they going hard, trying to take over our turf. Over my dead body, Blood. I need you to tell me everything you know about him from A to Z," PYT asked her sister.

Naya knew everything about him. She had even sat and had halal dinners with his Islamic family.

The two talked until the visit was over. They hated to say goodbye, but they planned a visit for another time.

PYT planned to meet China and spend some time with her before she headed back to New York.

Chapter 19
Somewhere in the Air

Rugar sat in the luxury G5 private jet he owned. He looked out the small round window into the clouds. The jet had a bedroom, two bathrooms, sixteen seats, a bar, a kitchen, laptops built into the walls, flat screens, personal waiters, and a pilot.

Savannah was still flashing in his head. He had no clue she was crazy. A sick part of his mind was somewhat turned on, but he would never risk his marriage.

"You okay, boss? You look tired," Tajada asked

"I'm fine, just need to spend some time with the family soon. Business been overwhelming," he told his head security guard. He was the leader of the five man crew he had with him at all times.

Tajada's name in English was Slice because he was well-trained with using knives on his enemies. He was born and raised in Artemisia, Cuba on the mean streets, where he robbed and killed to survive. Luckily, Jumbo gave him a second chance at life when he robbed and killed one of his workers. Jumbo had Tajada kidnapped and he was about to kill him at the young age of sixteen until he told him in Spanish he had to feed his sick mom, who died weeks later. Ever since then, Jumbo took him under his wing and groomed him into a deadly solider.

Rugar had plans to spend time with his family and take them to Disneyland but right, now he was about to land in New York.

***

Bronx

PYT sat in an empty Spanish restaurant in South Bronx, enjoying the Spanish comida. She had eight guards standing at the main entrance while three goons patrolled the area. Since her beef with the Muslims, she had to tighten security. She wore bulletproof vests and rode in bulletproof trucks with heavy artillery.

She had received a text from Patricia the other day asking her to meet with her so they could talk. PYT had liked Pat since the first time she met her and she was a big part of her company. She was a hard worker.

Pat walked through the door wearing a black Dior business suit with sunglasses on and her hair pinned up. The guards stopped her, about to search her, until they heard their boss's voice.

"She good," PYT said.

The guards had Pat nervous. She never saw PYT roll like this.

The two embraced like longtime friends and caught up for a few seconds.

"You hungry?" PYT asked.

"No, I'm okay," Pat said, taking off her blazer.

"Pruebe este safo (just taste this coffee)," PYT said.

"Sí," she replied as PYT told the waiter to bring her a cup of coffee

"How you been? I heard you got a billionaire investor. That's a good look. You may take Zoeman's place soon within the company," PYT stated as the coffee arrived.

"You know how I do: work hard play harder," Pat said.

"Muchas gracias," Pat told the Spanish waiter as he walked off to leave them alone.

"I'm here to tell you something important, since you saved my life," Pat said seriously.

PYT stopped eating upon seeing the fear in her eyes. Pat never had a clue what she was into. She figured it was scamming. But from the gruesome photos, she saw she knew it was far from scamming.

"What's wrong, Pat?" she asked. PYT had never seen her like this. She was normally joyful and excited.

"I've been dealing with a guy named Morris and he is a federal agent. We been dating on and off for some months now. So I was at his condo last week and I heard him mention PYT to himself while I was going to the bathroom. I stopped and asked him to repeat himself and he said PYT is the name of a person he's looking for who did a lot of murders. I almost shitted on myself. He's trying to connect you to some big murders with gang members," she said.

PYT began to eat her food as if it was nothing. "Do you love him, Pat?" she asked softly as if she was happy for them.

"Do money fall from the sky? You will always have my loyalty, PYT," she replied honestly.

They talked for a half hour and then went separate ways.

***

Port Chester

PYT walked in her home alone, hoping to take a long hot bubble bath. Brandon and the nanny were out with the security team at Playland Park.

She walked upstairs to hear her favorite Keith Sweat song playing low on the system in her bedroom. She pulled out her German 9mm and crept into her room, aiming her pistol at the figure laying roses on her bed.

"If you going to shoot, do it, love," Rugar said as he turned around. She looked good in her Louis Vuitton mesh dress and high heels.

"Sorry, baby," she said, lowering her gun and placing it back into her purse. She looked around her room to see candles, teddy bears, and roses.

The two hugged and kissed passionately

"I missed you so much. Come here," he said, picking up a tray of fresh cut up fruit with chocolate covering and peaches with cream in the middle of the tray.

"Ummm," she said as he fed her strawberries with chocolate swirls.

Rugar moved the roses off the bed and laid her down softly, kissing her neck while taking off her dress and underclothes. He only wore a robe and he was naked under it. He took it off, showing his chiseled frame and war wounds under his tattoos.

He sucked her hard nipples as she massaged his hard dick, horny like a cat in heat. Rugar made his way to his wife's pussy. He started to eat her small pussy, sucking on her hard clit as she moaned loudly while Keith Sweat sang in the background.

She grabbed his head and grinded her hips into his long tongue. He went crazy in her pussy, which smelled like cherries until she came on his face while he sucked her cum dry.

PYT switched places and got between his knees to be face to face with his full length dick. She started sucking the tip with her juicy lips. She was deep-throating him up and down while making loud slurping noises when she felt tears about to come out her eyes.

"Uhhh, shit," Rugar moaned as she sucked hard and deep until he couldn't take it anymore. He shot a big load in her mouth. She swallowed most of it, but the rest dripped out her mouth.

Rugar was ready to fuck. He placed her on top of him slowly because her walls were too tight and he could only get halfway in. They slow grinded to the music until he was inside of her all the way.

"Fuck me," she said, bouncing up and down like a cowgirl as her small titties bounced.

Rugar slammed her hips, into his going deeper.

"Uhhhh, fuck meeee, dadddyyyy!" she screamed as she felt him tearing her small phat pussy up.

Once they both came, he bent her on all four to see her ass spread wide, making it look huge, while her phat pussy poked out like a balloon.

He started to fuck her roughly as if there was no tomorrow. He ran in and out her warm wet pussy. It was so good that he had to squeeze his ass cheeks so he wouldn't nut.

"Shit, you hitting my spot," she moaned, biting the pillow and taking that dick as he dug her little walls out like a criminal.

"I'm cumming!" PYT yelled.

Rugar was about to also. He grabbed her small waist and fucked her harder and her body bounced back and forth like a rag doll.

They nutted. It was so heavy that cum was pouring out of her pussy. He pulled his dick out full of cum. PYT sucked all the cum off his dick, making his eyes roll back it felt so good.

Rugar was about to 69 with her until both of their emergency phones went off. They both ran to answer. The security team told them there was shooting near Playland Park and they rushed out of the house with their guns in hand.

Chapter 20
Playland Amusement Park

"Nanny, that was so cool! But I saw the look in your face when we was going down on the rollercoaster. You squeezed my hand so hard it hurts," Brandon said as they left Playland, walking into the parking lot.

"I'm so sorry, baby. I'm a little too old for the excitement. And its 98 degrees out here, boy. I know you hot," she said as the sun burned her smooth brown skin.

"Aunty said tomorrow we go to the movies," he said, taking a bite out of cotton candy, which was all over his face, hair, and hands.

"Of course," she said, looking behind her to see the four guards dressed in street clothes walking slowly, trying to blend in with the crowd. She already knew all their names by heart. She even slept with one, but then he started stalking her. That was the Spanish nigga. Monica was in her 40's but looked twenty. With her phat ass and pretty face, she would trick any man.

Once in the all-white Range Rover Sport truck, she placed Brandon in the car seat with a seatbelt, making sure he was strapped in as she always did.

"Thanks, Nanny," he said while hugging her with his little arms, making her laugh because he was too much.

"For what, baby?" she said looking into his little colorful eyes, knowing when he got older he was going to be a ladies' man.

"For having fun with me. I wish PYT and Rugar could come with us," he said falling asleep as she pulled off.

Before she could even answer or exit the parking lot, he was snoring. She knew he was tired. They had been up running around since six in the morning.

Monica couldn't wait to get home to prepare a big dinner for Rugar's arrival and the family plus the thirteen guards. She saw the guards two cars behind her in Yukon trucks. It was only a thirty minute ride back home so she played a Mary J Blige album to relax her mind.

Before she entered the gates, there was a loud explosion that almost made her crash head on with an all-black SUV speeding her way. She swerved left, hitting her brakes in the middle of the streets. Her head hit the steering wheel, knocking her unconscious while Brandon was still asleep.

One of the Yukon trucks was blown into pieces, killing both guards. Fire and smoke covered the roads while other cars reversed and got the fuck away.

Within seconds, shots started to ring out, which woke Monica up and made Brandon cry.

"Duck now, Brandon!" the nanny yelled as she grabbed her pistol out of her purse and crept out of the driver's seat.

The high-powered gun Malik and Bloody Ock carried turned the last guard into baked potatoes as bullets turned the truck into Swiss cheese in seconds before they could even hop out.

Monica shot at Malik, hoping to hit him, but she missed every shot. She tried to run, but bullets went through her back, stomach, lungs, kidneys, and liver, killing her before she could make it to the Range.

Malik and Bloody Ock knew the Range was PYT's, but they knew the lady on the ground wasn't her. They had been watching the white Range with tints for three days, thinking it was PYT.

Malik and Bloody Ock ran to the truck, hoping she was in there, but they only saw a little kid with colorful eyes trying to hold his tears back, feeling a pain in his leg.

"Should I?" Bloody Ock said, ready to kill.

"No. Let's go!" Malik yelled as they rushed back to the SUV, pulling off as sirens sounded a block away. "That was the wrong damn person!" Malik yelled, hitting the steering wheel, knowing that hit had been too easy.

"Damn, ock," Bloody Ock stated not knowing who the bitch was they had killed.

The two had followed the Range all morning thanks to his pops giving him PYT's address and type of car she was driving, but little did they know she had two white Ranges. Once they went in Playland, Bloody Ock placed a small device that was a bomb under one of the guard's trucks. The plan was to place it under the Range, but Malik wanted to take PYT out himself. He loved a challenge.

The two men rode in silence to their new hideout in Brooklyn, but they couldn't get the kid in the Range off their minds.

***

Brooklyn, Brownsville

"You know this is going to be a big issue. We missed our target," Malik stated.

Bloody Ock walked with him into the basement of the Brooklyn mosque to see Muhammad.

Muhammad heard his door open, which made him smile because he was waiting on the news of PYT's death. The bitch was a psychopath.

"I'm sorry, Father, we missed. It wasn't her."

"What?" Muhammad yelled as he banged his fist on the wooden table, kicking over the incense onto the floor. "Next time there won't be no sorry. Both of you will be answering for it. Now get the fuck out!" Muhammad shouted pissed off.

"I think this shit about to get a little crazy," Bloody Ock said, following Malik upstairs

"Me too, but I'ma make it right. Let's pray, then I got a plan," he said falling into line while the Muslims made there last prayer of the day.

***

Bronx

"Ohhh, uhhhh, damn, nigga!" Cherry screamed. Murder had her legs over her ears, long-stroking her as she came four times.

"Mmmm," Murder moaned. He came in her waterfall as she worked her pussy muscle. "Damn, that was a good quickie. I'll be back for the real shit later, I gotta go meet Red Hat, boo," he said as she sucked her teeth, covering up her thick body.

"Why don't you go legit, baby, and open up some more auto body shops? My brother doing life in the feds for drugs," she said seriously.

"Babe, I will soon. We in a war now. I promise after this ends, I'm out," he said kissing her before he left.

Cherry laid in bed in deep thought, thinking about her future and the future of the unborn seed growing in her stomach. She never told Murder that she could get pregnant easily. That was why she always used condoms, even in the clubs, but it was what it was now.

Chapter 21
Federal Women's Prison

Naya was in the day room playing dominos with a couple of Spanish women who gambled for money all day. Most women in the unit were serving life sentences as well

"Damn, how the fuck you always win?" Big Gee said, pulling out 800 dollars in stamps and passing it to Naya.

"You can win it back after count time. I'ma give you half on the come out, Jazzy," said Naya, walking off to her cell. Luckily Cat was at work so she placed a blocker on the cell door window.

She had called home yesterday to find out her son was shot in his leg. She was pissed, unable to eat and sleep, worrying about his safety. She knew he was safe in the presence of his aunt and uncle, but she knew no one could protect a child like his mother.

The nanny was murdered, but she heard she went out like a true gangsta from New York. She was always thankful to have Monica in her life. Rugar explained the whole story. She was just glad her son was okay. He was supposed to come see her next week, but she planned it for next month. She had to get him on her visit list.

Naya heard a light knock at the door

"Wait!" she yelled from her bunk.

"Sorry to disturb you, but your husband is here to see you," the female C.O. said with her colorful hair and long manicured nails.

"A'ight" Naya said. She grabbed her shower bag and the nine inch knife she made out of her steel bed and went upstairs to take a shower for her visit.

***

Ronell sat in the visiting room waiting on Naya. He had heard about the shooting with her son. China kept him posted through Pressure.

The prison had been on lock down the last couple of days because a woman stabbed another woman to death over a nacho bowl so he couldn't visit her last weekend. But he refused to miss this one.

Naya walked into the visit room and hugged him.

"You okay, baby?" he asked.

"I'm okay," she said flatly.

"Look, I'ma find out who is behind this. I love you and I'm here for you," he said.

"I love you too. How's life?" she asked.

The two talked the whole visit about everything until it was over.

***

Atlanta, GA

Pressure and Glizzy posted up in the gentlemen's club in zone 6. The two had been good friends for years. Glizzy ran the "A" and Pressure was a guest in his city, but he also had a serious crew moving weight on the west side.

"How's Miami, bro? I heard you got the city on lock. I went down there last week and a bitch asked me who did I know. I didn't want to name drop, but I told her I was somebody. The bitch tells me, 'well, you're nobody if you not down with Pressure and his crew.' So I told her I was in town to see you and I fucked the Cuban bitch all night. Her shit was fire," Glizzy said, laughing and drinking out of a large bottle of Cirôc.

"I bet you paid for it too," Pressure said, knowing Miami bitches.

"Of course, fam, why not?" Glizzy said, watching the strippers get crazy on stage.

"You heard of a nigga named Rugar?" Pressure asked, knowing Glizzy was from New York and affiliated with the Bloods up there because he controlled the Bloods in Atlanta.

"Yeah, why? That was the big homie before he passed," Glizzy said sadly.

"He's alive. He came to Miami to see my wifey China. I heard he a stand-up dude," Pressure said.

100

Glizzy thought it was another person he was talking about. "I think - hold on, China? You fuck with China?" Glizzy said, remembering how he had a crush on her as a kid, but Brazy and Rugar weren't going for it.

"Yeah, that's wifey. You know her?" Pressure asked not knowing Glizzy was in the same circle he was now in.

"I grew up with her. But I gotta make a call to up top to see if I'm hearing you correct because Rugar been dead," Glizzy said. He called Red Hat, talking in code for a couple of minutes while Pressure watched his goons toss bands on stage.

"Damn, this shit crazy. That was him. I can't believe it," Glizzy said, surprised when Red Hat told him Rugar was back.

"Yeah, I saw him," Pressure said.

"This shit about to be crazy now," Glizzy said.

The rest of the night went smoothly until someone got shot in a shootout in the parking lot over a parking space.

Chapter 22
Downtown Brooklyn

Bam Bam sat in Skyline Studio with twenty goons all bopping their heads to K-Roc freestyling over a Fabolus beat, killing it in the booth.

"The homies know I keep an AK on the block fully loaded clip rundown and you can get shot. Red Chucks, red Balmains on the block where it's hot, fuck a Fed, fuck a cop. I'm from Brooklyn where niggas run down on an op. I'm the king of Brooklyn; since Biggie left I have his spot." K-Roc spit fire bars in the booth as the studio went crazy.

K-Roc was the best thing coming out of Brooklyn. He was signed to Bam Bam's record label Skyline Records. Bam Bam started the label years ago. He started from the ground up to clean all his dirty money with the help of some lawyers.

"Yo, son, I like that shit. We gotta put that shit on a mixtape," Bam Bam said as K-Roc came out of the booth with his chain swinging on his 6'5" basketball player frame.

"I'm cool with that, my nigga. But I'ma head out to this club," K-Roc said, snatching a bottle out of a groupie bitch's hand and drinking it.

Bam Bam laughed until he saw a bunch of masked men run up in the spot with guns firing. Bodies were dropping left and right as both crews had a vicious gun battle.

K-Roc hid behind a thick bitch as bullets hit her over twenty times. He tried to run, but the four wild bullets to the neck and face paused him.

Malik saw K-Roc's body and saw Bam Bam taking out most of his men alone while two of his goons held him down.

"Blood, I'm almost out!" Fearless B shouted, covering Bam Bam and shooting at the masked men while Bam Bam was still taking them out left and right.

"What the fuck, Blood?" said Bam Bam as Bloody Ock took out his two guards, leaving him naked as he went to hide behind speakers. They were outnumbered. There was so much blood and smoke in the air that Bam Bam got dizzy. He dipped into the fire exit as bullets flew past his head.

Bloody Ock and Malik were the only barefaced Muslims. The other four left standing were covered. They all chased Bam Bam's ass out the exit until they made it outside and all they saw was a Benz taillight speeding down the dark streets of Brooklyn.

***

Washington Height

PYT had just left Red Hat's condo in the Heights, where the Dominican was selling drugs and playing cards and dominos all day.

Red Hat had a nice condo with two beautiful Spanish women - Lyric and Yasmine - who were his ride or die chicks. Both of the women hated PYT because he treated her better than them and showed her respect. They always had fake smiles when she came around because they saw her in action one day and wanted no parts of it.

"Papi, you okay?" Lyric asked, sitting on the king-sized bed. The sun brightened the room while she rubbed his shoulders in her bra and panties with her ass and breasts busting out.

"Yeah, you don't look too well," Yasmine said as she laid in his lap, rubbing his thighs, ready to suck his dick.

"Yeah, but we gotta handle some shit tonight, so go get dressed," he said.

Both women hopped up, rushing out of the room, asses bouncing and shaking, ready to do as he demanded.

***

New Jersey

Sister Maria walked around inside Toys R Us with her children as the Muslim guards waited outside

"Mommy, can we please get a swimming pool? It's getting hot. Please?" Young Khalid asked, walking past the pool section.

"Let me ask your father first." Maria was dressed in her Muslim gear and covered from head to toe. She was thirty-six, chubby with a wide ass and nice long real hair. At 5'11" and 198 pounds, she was still cute.

Maria was a full time mom. Since Muhammad was never around to help with his kids - he had so many and so much shit going on - she just played her part. She didn't mind being a housewife. She had signed up for it and was ready to go through whatever trials her marriage had planned for her.

***

A black truck filled with four linebackers with dreads sat in the Toys R Us lot. As they were waiting they saw two beautiful women walk past them wearing leggings, asses hanging out, toward a gray Benz.

The two women were walking around the Benz as if something was wrong. One of them popped the trunk and bent over, showing her ass and phat pussy from the back. The other one squatted down as if something was wrong with the tires.

"Damn, she phat to death," the large driver said loudly, not realizing everyone heard him

"What you say?" one of the guards said from the back, watching the scene.

Yasmine and Lyric were putting on a show for the men. They grabbed their purses out of the Benz and walked off, looking around as if they were looking for help. Once they laid eyes on the men in the truck they smiled and walked in their direction, causing a traffic jam in the lot. When the Muslim guards saw them coming, they all rolled down their windows as if they hadn't been staring the whole time

"Excuse me, gentlemen, but me and my girl not from around here and we caught a flat. Can you help us?" Yasmine asked.

Lyric approached the other window, and all four men couldn't help but stare at them.

"Ahem," the driver said, clearing his throat, "I'm sure we can help. Do you have the extra tire?" he asked, staring at her large breasts.

"Yes I do, and I promise me and my girl will make it up to you," Yasmine said.

"We will make you very happy," Lyric added.

"Okay, one second," the driver said, looking at all the brothers in the truck as they nodded and told him to hurry up.

Before he could even turn around, Lyric shot both the driver and passenger in the head while Yasmine took out the two in the back seat. Their pistols had silencers so they could muffle the gunshots. They walked off smoothly, swaying their hips as if they wanted attention as they climbed in the Benz and circled the lot.

***

Maria walked through the lot and made it to her Cadillac truck parked in the middle of the lot. She placed all the bags in the backseat with her kids as she normally did. She was sure the guards had seen her come out. It was time to go.

As soon as she started the truck, Red Hat popped up from the back trunk area and shot her in the back of the head three times. The kids started to scream until he placed bullets in their little kufis.

Red Hat climbed out of the truck and took the silencer off the pistol. He saw the Benz pull up slowly and he hopped in smoothly. They hit the highway, heading to the New Jersey tunnel while a Meek Mill album played in the background.

Yasmine was driving. Lyric was in the backseat sucking Red Hat's dick while looking him in his eyes until he busted down her throat.

PYT came up with that idea when she went to go meet him, and he had to admit that she was playing for keeps. Since Lil Brazy got shot, she played by no rules. He had just killed three kids, but he had no remorse. It was a cold game.

He played with Lyric's phat juicy pussy while Yasmine watched, thirsty to get home to she could suck some dick and get some pussy.

Chapter 23
Miami, FL

Ronell stood on his condo balcony near South Beach, looking over the city in deep thought, waiting on Pressure. Lately he been in the gym working out hard to relieve some stress, and his arms and chest had blown up as if he was lifting weights on the Allenwood USP yards as he did years ago during his bid.

Pressure had just walked into his condo. He was on the phone discussing business in code with his client about the keys that his mule got caught with last night after a big police chase on his way to Crashville. The mule was able to toss two duffle bags that each contained thirty-five keys of coke into a river, but he and the passenger were still caught with seven keys of dope and two loaded AK-47 assault rifles in the trunk. The crazy part was that the passenger, G-Baby, was said to be released on a $250,000 bail that was given to him within hours, unlike his friend, who was being held without bail. G-Baby claimed his cousin in the NBA bailed him out, someone nobody had heard of before.

Pressure was a street nigga that knew the law, unlike most street niggas, so he knew if you got caught with drugs and guns with a rap sheet, there was no chance of bail - at least until you saw a judge the next day.

"What's good, shawty?" Pressure asked, walking out on the large balcony, enjoying the hot Miami heat and cool ocean breeze.

"Chilling, my nigga. Getting ready to meet with this crazy bitch today," Ronell said, referring to his connect, Katie.

"You need me to come?" Pressure asked, sitting down.

"Nah, go handle your business. I got it. But slide out to Tampa and holla at Moe and that Rich kid to see about that spot for me to set up a new club. Tampa is a gold mine," Ronell said.

"Okay, I got you," Pressure said.

"One more thing. Reach out to your New York niggas and figure out who's responsible for Naya's son being shot," Ronell said, thinking about Naya.

"Got you. China told me something about that. I'ma handle it," Pressure said, standing to leave.

"No, I'ma handle it. You just find out who I gotta reach," Ronell said, facing the city he loved the most.

***

Katie entered the club with eight large henchmen, all of them white with bald heads and tattoos as if they were Nazis in suits. Wherever she went, there was security with her and lurking all over to protect their boss.

Katie was young, rich, freaky, controlling, sexy, and very dangerous. She was from the UK, but she traveled daily. Her favorite spot was the United States, especially Miami. She loved the nightlife, and Miami was the best besides Vegas.

She was 5'3" in height with blue eyes and long blonde hair. She was petite with a round ass and small breasts. Her pussy and nipples were pierced as well as her nose, tongue, and dimples. She looked like a Barbie doll instead of a leader of a powerful cartel that controlled the drug and weapon trades in the UK.

Ronell's club was packed, loud, and live. People were dancing sexually, standing on couches in the middle of the floor, bottle popping and enjoying themselves. Katie walked through the club in a white, extra tight Christian Dior dress with no bra or panties. It was so tight and short she had to keep pulling it down to keep her ass cheeks out of sight.

She saw Ronell alone in VIP. There were two ice buckets filled of ice and Louis Vuitton 13 and Moët from France especially ordered. She smiled when she saw him and rushed to give him a hug. The two had a good friendship.

The two had met years ago. They slept with each other once and then after that it, was strictly business. He needed a connect, and she was it. Normally Katie was known for killing the men she slept with for the fun of it, but the way Ronell made love to her with his big black dick, she fell for him. She loved blacks. She hated white men. They were a turn off to her. Blacks were beautiful to her.

"You look amazing," Ronell said as they both sat down while her guards posted outside the ropes.

"Thanks. Nice place. It looks different," she said in her strong UK accent that sounded sexy to most.

"Something easy, not too much. Champagne or wine?"

"Both. But before I forget, congratulations on your marriage. You're a married man now," she said.

He looked surprised because he wasn't even wearing his wedding band. "Thanks. But how you find out?" he asked, pouring her a glass of Moët.

She smiled, showing her bright white teeth as the dim lights hit her icy watch and necklace. "I have long connections, Ronell, and I keep tabs on you, my friend. We are like family," she said, sipping on her drink and watching the club get crazy to a Pitbull song

"True. But how has life been for you, beautiful?" he asked.

"Great. I'ma be out here for the weekend, so I'm staying at your place. Make room, player, and no touching or looking. You're married now," Katie said, smiling. She always stayed with him and they would chill and watch TV or go out to clubs. It was never about sex or lust. They had a real bond.

"As long as you cook that pasta shit you made last time. I'd rather jerk off than fuck you," he said, making her laugh because the first and last time he had some of her goods, he was moaning her name like a bitch, her pussy and head game were so good.

"I bet. But how's business? I'm going to ship the new shipment to Alabama, Mobile at the same spot in two days, so have your people come correct because last time, you shorted me two hundred, wise ass," Katie said.

"No I deducted two hundred from our last dinner that I paid for," he said.

"Okay, petty ass," she said bopping her head to a Drake song.

"The prices have been lower lately. What's up with that?"

"Yeah, there are new leaders in the head chair of the Cartel. They're young and beautiful, I must say, and the wife is very deadly - my type of bitch. But they playing fair, so I can play fair with you," she said.

"I hope they keep it at this rate, shit!" Ronell said.

"I got faith in them. But hey, let's dance. I love this Chris Brown song," Katie said, grabbing his hand as she stood up, tipsy and ready to party.

She got on the dance floor and grinded on Ronell's dick all night. For a white girl raised in a rich family, she acted like a ghetto white chick.

Chapter 24
New York City

Agent Morris drove in his work car, an all-black Crown Vic with tints, on his way home from a sixteen hour shift. The city had so many homicides lately that the NYPD and DEA were sending caseloads to the FBI for help. What Agent Morris realized was all the brutal murders going on there had so much in common. Dead Muslims, ex-cons, Blood gang members...and it seemed as if there was an underworld turf war going on. The FBI hadn't seen so many murders in years and his captain was still on bullshit, telling him to stay down. The captain recently informed the media that he was cracking down on gangs, drugs, and violence within the city, but there were still no arrests. Morris received a file on his desk a couple of weeks ago about a family of Muslims being murdered in a studio in Brooklyn. He knew he was close to cracking the biggest case of his career and there was no way he was staying down.

Yesterday he came across a case where a forty-year-old woman was murdered in a shootout and a child was shot at the scene. There was something about the case that attracted his attention. A truck was blown up and there were four dead security guards at the scene from Cuba with no green cards.

Monica dying with a pistol in her hand was crazy to him, so he did some research into her and the little kid that was shot. When the background check came back, Monica was clean, but the kid's mother was a queenpin who had been sentenced to life in prison. He remembered her big story in the media. He saw a name on the kid's birth certificate that sent a shock wave through his brain. His father was Brazy. Morris had spent years trying to find any evidence so he could charge him, but he was too smart - until he killed some Crips in broad daylight.

After days of piecing everything together, he came to realize that Naya was somehow related to the woman he been hunting for months. When he saw PYT come out of the hospital days ago, his stomach flipped. He tried to tail her, but the all-red Jaguar moved swiftly through traffic like a bat at night, leaving him in the wind.

He didn't figure out why all the murders in the city were happening, but he knew it was something big. Tonight he wasn't going to sleep until he got down to the nitty gritty.

***

Once in his downtown apartment, he placed his keys and gun on his kitchen counter. He had a nice pad with two bedrooms, but he used one room for his personal office. When he wasn't at work, this was his life.

He grabbed a cranberry juice out of the freezer and walked into his living room. He sat on the couch and turned on his flat screen TV to watch the daily world news as he did every night.

After an hour of news, it was time to work, He walked to his bedroom to get into something comfortable. He heard movement in his bedroom. Normally Patricia would surprise him dressed up in different freaky outfits. She had a spare key, so it was nothing for her to get in.

"Pat? Is that you, baby?" he said, feeling his dick grow instantly. He turned on the lights because it was pitch black.

When the lights came on, he froze. He saw the most beautiful woman he ever saw dressed in a Chanel black mini dress with Miu Miu heels on, legs crossed, doing something on his computer.

"Good evening, Mr. Morris," PYT said, turning around in the rolling chair, now facing him, showing her nice smooth legs.

"You got two seconds to explain who the fuck you are and what you're doing in my house!" he shouted while trying to get a better look at her.

"Okay, big shot agent. I'm PYT, your dream girl. I'm here, so you can stop trying figure out who I am and stop trying to tail me from the hospital," she said, laughing as she stood with a loaded cannon so big he almost choked on his spit.

He got a good look at her to see she was indeed PYT. He thought about his gun in the kitchen and the one under his bed, but he knew his chances of getting to them were zero to one.

"I see you're very surprised. But that's not the best part. It gets better," she said, smiling as he stood there with his mind racing.

Patricia walked out of the bathroom wearing a hoodie sweat-suit with a small gun in her hand that belonged to him.

"Pat, what the fuck? What's going on?" he said, hurt.

"Morris, please stop with the crybaby shit. You're making yourself look dumb. You was just a super agent hours ago, now you turning into a bitch," Patricia said, shaking her head. "PYT is like a sister to me, so when I saw you trying to build a case on her, I had to protect her," Patricia said, looking at PYT while they both had him at gunpoint.

"You two bitches will never get away with this. My boss will have your asses fried in the electric chair!' Morris yelled.

"Too bad your boss wanted you dead more than me. He said you was a headache. You see, you barked up the wrong tree. I run a cartel family and your boss is the brother of the Mexican Cartel, so we all family, just different races - all bonded by money," PYT stated, smiling and checking her watch.

He was confused. This was bigger than he thought. But he knew if he made it out of this, his boss would be the first one he built charges on.

"Fuck! I knew I was onto something!" he shouted, grabbing his spiky hair.

"Yeah, but nice catching up. I'm sure we'll cross paths in hell at the lowest level."

Boom! Boom! Boom! Both women filled his body with rounds.

"Do we just leave him here?" Pat asked, watching him die with his eyes open.

"No, don't worry, he will have company," PYT said.

It took Pat a minute to figure out what she meant

Bloc! Bloc!

Pat's frail body hit the floor with a loud thump as two bullet entered skull.

PYT walked out of the room to the kitchen, where she had a rope tied to the fire escape hanging to the ground to avoid cameras and witnesses. She really liked Pat, but she knew she had said too much to her about the Cartel, plus she didn't trust no nigga or bitch.

***

Miami, FL

"Make sure you talk about prices, murders, drugs, guns, connects...shit, talk about taxes, we don't care. Just enough to get him, please. He thinks he's smart, but we got him now. We ain't get you out of jail for nothing, G-Baby. Just know if you don't do this, you could go to prison for a long time," Agent Blackmen stated as he sat in the surveillance van two blocks away from where he was supposed to meet Pressure.

G-Baby was sweating and shaking as they placed a wire with tape on his hairy chest. He grew up in Liberty City with Pressure. He worked for him for years. The Feds had been on G-Baby for six months, but he could never lead them to Pressure, so they caught him on the highway with Loon. They tried to get Loon to break, but he wouldn't fold. He was a real stand-up street nigga and Pressure was a good nigga. When he went to jail, Pressure held his family down financially for three years.

"Okay, I understand," he said feeling the wire and thinking about either dropping the soap in a USP or telling on Pressure, and Pressure it was.

"Good luck. Now get the fuck out, snitch," Agent Blackmen said, laughing with his partner, Agent Ferg.

***

Overtown, Miami

G-Baby hopped out of the van, walking down a block near North Boulevard, As soon as he spun the block, he saw an all-white '95 Impala sitting on 28 inch rims blasting a Yo Gotti album.

Pressure pulled up to the curb and picked him up. They were driving through the hood to see goons posted on the block with dreads and gold mouths.

"What's good, bruh-bruh? Shit crazy! I'm glad I made bail. I tossed most of the work. They should give Loon bail this week," G-Baby said.

Pressure just nodded his head to the loud music. He pulled into an abandoned building's parking lot. There were no street lights, so it was dark outside.

"Check this spot out. I want to rent it and turn it into a home-less shelter!" Pressure shouted over the loud music.

"Did you hear from Meech? I got niggas who need fifty keys from Palm Beach ASAP and I'ma hit you back on them keys we lost." G-Baby was waiting on a reply.

"Help me with this, cuz." Pressure parked and pulled out a gas container and walked around to his trunk. Pressure threw the gas on his chest, soaking him, believing that gasoline would disable a wire or interfere with it if G-Baby was wearing one.

"What the fuck!" G-Baby shouted until he saw a 50 cal pistol pointed at his face.

"You rat-ass nigga! What you tell them people?" Pressure yelled.

"Nothing yet. They trying to get me to set you up, bruh. I was going to tell you. Please, I got kids, man. I love you, bruh. We go way back."

Pressure shot him six times in his upper torso, then jumped back in his car listen to Yo Gotti on his way to give Keisha money to bail Loon out.

Chapter 25
Cuba

Rugar flew back to Cuba this morning to handle some business affairs with Katie and Juda and he had plans to get up with Jumbo. Rugar walked into the backyard wearing a fitted V-neck Versace shirt and shorts to match his loafers and sunglasses. His muscles were bulky since he got on his workout shit again weeks ago. He did three days of weightlifting and two days of intense cardio.

Business had been crazy lately and his personal family issues didn't help, but he still knew how to separate the two.

"Good to see you, nephew. I heard what happened to Lil Brazy. Don't forget to use your muscle and power. That's why it's here," Jumbo stated, sipping grapefruit juice as he saw Rugar coming outside.

"I know. But you don't look too well," Rugar said, sitting next to him to see that he lost a gang of weight due to the cancer.

The maid walked outside to give Jumbo his lunch and medicine.

"Creo que tomora un poco de sopa (I'll think I'll try some soup)," Jumbo said softly to her as she walked off to prepare his meal. To Rugar, he said, "I'm good, kid. Waiting on our visitors. I'm having Hagor prepare a big meal later."

"I believe Ms. Costilla Alvers is supposed to come also instead of Juda. He canceled at the last moment," Rugar stated.

"Juda is good for business, but you just can't trust his type. Katie and Costilla are the main consumers. Make sure security is tight at meetings, because those two women are very dangerous and deadly - trust me," Jumbo said, being honest and schooling him.

"I already did my research. The security team is in position and I plan to take the women out for a little fun." Rugar watched Savannah climb out of the pool in a bikini with her long hair wet and curly. His dick got hard as he looked at the thin string bunched in her shaved, smooth, thin pussy lips.

"Hola papi and Mr. Rugar. Sorry to hear about your nephew's shooting," she said as the sun bounced off her smooth, soft skin. "Papi, are you okay?" she said, noticing he looked weak.

"Yes. Let me talk in private. Put some clothes on and go attend to the soldiers."

She listened and left with an attitude. She put an extra swing in her hips, walking off. She hadn't seen Rugar in days and wanted to show him what he was missing.

"That girl is too sneaky for her own good. Just do me a favor, kid. Watch out for her, kid, because I know if given the chance, she will destroy everything we built. No matter what, water will never be equal to blood, so with that said, if she ever crosses the line, kill her," Jumbo said.

Rugar nodded his head, wondering if he should tell him about the crazy scene he had with her. He looked at the mansion to see her staring out a bedroom window at him before quietly closing the curtains.

"You remind me so much of Chilli. She had the heart of a tiger, but she was a caring woman, and in this game, caring is a weakness. When the Lord, Allah, Jesus, whoever comes for me soon, I'ma go in peace. But take care of everything I left. Never let nobody take what you worked so hard to build. I had a lot of people try to take what I built," Jumbo said, pointing at his chest.

They spent an hour talking about business and Jumbo schooled him on the cartel.

***

Dinner was amazing overall. Costilla and Katie were good company. The women even helped cook. The dinner had everything from Spanish food to soul food. Savannah looked amazed and Hagor looked even better.

Savannah was jealous that Rugar was giving the two women too much entertainment. She had a plan for them. There was no way she was going to be played. What Rugar didn't know was that Savannah was very emotional, and that could be dangerous.

***

After dinner, Rugar, Katie, and Costilla all got into the bullet-proof Hummer truck followed by five trucks of goons as they rode through the streets of Mayabeque.

"So how do you like the new seat?" Katie asked in her British accent.

"It's great. All the families can come together and get money and build trust," Rugar stated, looking out the window of the passenger side while the women sat in the back.

Katie had to admit Rugar was handsome. He was about his business, and that made her pussy wet, but she knew he was married.

"True, and I must say, I respect the way you do business. It's different from what I have seen, but very smooth, witty, and thought out like a true New Yorker," Costilla said.

Costilla was a head turner. At the age of forty-two, she looked twenty. She was model material with long black hair, thick curves, a flat tummy from lipo, and a youthful face. She ran the Colombia Cartel with an iron fist. There were only four women who ran cartel families, and she was one of them.

***

Once inside the packed nightclub, they had their own VIP area full of Spanish alcohol and strong wine for the women. The club played Latina music. This was the finest club in the city with two levels and bubbles falling from the ceiling.

"I think we should turn pure coca leaves into pills instead of powder. It would be easy to move and stronger. I had my scientist do some tests and it came out great. I just need the family's support. One key of coke is 100 pills. This is a big investment and upgrade to us," Rugar stated.

Costilla and Katie were amazed because traveling with pills instead of coke would be easier and safer.

"I'm down. Hell yeah! I see billions already," Katie said, fixing her bra inside her Versace gown.

"I'm down if it's true what you are saying," Costilla said in her strong Spanish accent.

"I will never lie to you. I'll have my men ship orders to your given location so you can see for yourself," he said.

"Okay, good. How's your wife? I like her. She did some work for my brother years ago before I had to kill him. She is very talented," Costilla stated.

"I've heard the same, and she is very beautiful," Katie said, drinking wine and enjoying the club scene with its dancing lights.

"She is well, thank you for asking. She is a blessing."

"I have to use the restroom," Costilla stated. She stood up in her classy wrap designer dress and heels, all Alberta Ferretti

"I'ma go with her. This wine is kicking my ass," Katie said, following.

Rugar stood to follow them.

"You can chill. We're big girls, and we have twenty-something men in here," Katie said as he sat down.

"Okay," he said, pulling out his phone and texting PYT to check on her.

Inside the small bathroom, there were mirrors posted all over the walls and five stalls with an open window. Something seemed off to the two women.

"That's odd," Katie said as she saw that all the bathroom doors were shut. Normally in clubs some are open because who would take a shit in a club restroom? And five people at once was odd.

Before either of them could open the stall doors, two masked men dressed in all black hopped out and attacked them.

Costilla was the first to react, doing a front side kick, dropping one of them. Katie ducked as the other attacker swung his knife blade at her head. She was able to kick the knife out of his hand and punch him in his throat, making him fall backwards into the bathroom sink while another masked man came in from the open window.

Costilla attacked with a seven piece combination, knocking him out and then snapping his neck with her hands. Katie took a two piece powerful hit to the stomach, doubling back, which made her mad. She pulled out two blades from under her dress.

"Bitch, bring it on!" she yelled, rushing him, stabbing in his heart multiple at the speed of light. His body went into shock, dying on her knife.

Rugar rushed in the restroom with ten guards to see both women in the mirror fixing their hair and makeup, standing on the dead bodies for a boost.

"What the fuck?" Rugar shouted, pissed off that his guest get attacked in his presence. It made him look like less of a man.

"Where we off to now, papi?" Costilla said, walking out of the bathroom as if nothing happened with Katie behind her.

"Clean this shit up now," Rugar told the guards who were supposed to be watching them closely.

They left the club and hit up a couple more clubs before going back to stay at Rugar's guest house until they both flew out in the morning.

Chapter 26
Manhattan, NY

"Mr. Martina, I can assure you we will find Agent Morris's killer. There's no doubt in my mind that my men will do anything to catch his murderer. Just give me some time," Mr. Lopez told his boss, who was the head of the FBI.

"I'm sure you will, because Washington is up my ass like a stiff dick." Mr. Martina sat sitting behind his desk in his large office, which had a skyrise view of the city.

Mr. Martina was an African-American from New Jersey. He had been an agent for thirty years; now he was pushing fifty in two weeks. He had a large family, but most of his kids became drug users and jailbirds.

When the news of Agent Morris hit the airwaves, the media ate it alive. It was a nasty situation, but luckily none of it traced back to him. He had been planning to kill Morris himself when PYT paid him a visit at his home, informing him of what Pat told her. PYT told him she would handle it. But he had no clue she was going to have his body disposed of in pieces and shipped to a police precinct's doorstep.

Luckily, PYT had Pat's body disposed of in Queens somewhere inside of a dumpster. That night she had gathered all of his files and records off his computer and loaded it on to his hard drive and took it as well as all documents leading to her or the Empire.

"I gotta get back to work across town. I'll keep you posted. Everything will be taken care of." Lopez stood up to leave.

"Make me happy, because obviously, as you see, I'm not," Mr. Martina said with a frown.

"Yes sir, I will," he said, walking out and letting his boss get back to work.

***
Brooklyn, NY

"Yooo, we got the truck loaded. Everything is ready, Blood," said Blake. He walked up to Bam Bam, who was standing in the back parking lot waiting for his man to give him the word.

Bam Bam had been laying low since the shootout with the Muslims in his studio, which was now closed down. He lost a lot of good men that night. He thought about that night daily, but seeing Bloody's face...that fucked him up.

He and Bloody Ock grew up together. They were close, but when Bloody Ock caught his case, they went different ways in life. Bam Bam joined the Empire and got rich thanks to Brazy, his young boy. He heard Bloody turned into a real Muslim and he never heard from him again or saw him until the studio shootout.

Since the shooting, Bam Bam had been laying low in Mount Vernon with some of his homies, but he had his goons at every mosque in the city looking for Muhammad, especially on Fridays.

"A'ight, Blood," Bam Bam said while talking on the phone. Once he hung up, he grabbed two pistols with an extendo clip attached to the bottom handles.

"Let's ride!" he yelled as he climbed in the back seat of a Yukon GMC truck full of strapped up goons.

***

Harlem

The mosque was semi-crowded today, but not as it normally was on weekdays. Most families prayed on the thick carpet while some read.

The mosque was a two-story building with a large praying area as soon as you walked in. There were private quite rooms, two kitchens, four bathrooms, and a children's area with Islamic kids' books.

Bloody Ock and Big Neefe guarded the mosque in Harlem most of the time because Muhammad and Young Malik were always in Jersey, Philly, or D.C.

Bloody Ock sat in one of the private rooms and read the Noble Quran in Arabic, trying to clear his mind and prepare for his first marriage tomorrow. Months ago he met a beautiful high yellow Muslim woman from London and the two were ready to get married. He was reading Surah 2 Al-Baqorah verse 228-232 and 223 about marriages and wives. He was still on parole so he had a 9 p.m. curfew in Brooklyn where he lived. It was 7:30 p.m. He figured he could read two more chapters, then have one of the brothers drive him home.

As soon as he was about to turn the page, he heard gunfire and screams. He jumped up and grabbed the SK assault rifle by the door, ready for jihad on a disbeliever.

***

Bam Bam and his men ran into the mosque firing, no holds barred, killing kids, women, and the elders. The place was so big it was hard to find who they were there for, so they spread out.

Big Neefe had a shotgun with double barrels shooting at the gunmen while cowering behind a wall

"You come into the house of Allah with this shit?" Neefe shouted, coming from around the corner and shooting three of the gunmen in the stomachs as the rest ran around trying to take the big man out.

Four Muslim women ran out of the kitchen shooting towards the gunmen, taking them out. These women were trained shooters. Muhammad had all of them go to a gun range upstate twice a week with the Muslim men.

Bam Bam and two of his men hid behind a wall, going bullet for bullet with the women, wondering what type of high power rifle they had because it was taking chunks off the walls.

"Fuck, we gotta kill these desert bitchs," Bam Bam said as they just stood in the middle of the floor, waiting for Bam Bam and his crew behind the wall while Big Neefe was shooting it out with five of his gunmen.

Sick of playing cat and mouse, Bam Bam came from his spot, shooting taking two of them out while his men hit the other women in the head.

"Allah Akbar!" Big Neefe yelled as bullets ripped through his chest and legs from behind. He was unaware some more Bloods sneaked in through the back door.

Bloody Ock came out of nowhere, shooting like a trained assassin, taking out most of them because they had their backs turned, unaware anybody was in the small private room.

Tat-tat-tat, BOOM! BOOM! Bloc! Tat-tat, BOOM!

"Get close on him! Close him in now!" Bam Bam yelled, realizing he had got hit in the vest, which took the wind out of him. He sat down with his back to a wall.

More women came out with pistols, moving like ninjas at night, zig-zagging like they were in a video game.

Two shooters saw the women ducking on the side of the wall near the bathroom. Bloody Ock saw it from a distance. He shot one of the men while the women saw the deadly move and shot the other man between his eyes.

The two women thought it was over and put down their weapons.

"Noooo!" Bloody Ock yelled as bullets hit both women's bodies as if it was for target practice.

Bloody sprayed his SK at the two men who killed the last two Muslims, taking them out.

"I told you I'll see you again, nigga! You couldn't even send a nigga a letter up north!" he yelled, looking around to see if there were any gunmen left.

"Fuck you! I know you still eat pork!" Bam Bam yelled, seeing his shadow wondering, if he could catch him without getting hit. Before he knew it or could make a move, Bloody Ock had his gun directly in his face as soon as he looked around the corner.

"Stand up like a real man," Bloody Ock said as Bam Bam followed orders

Bloc! Bloc! Bloc! Bloc!

Bullets hit Bloody Ock in his lower back, dropping him to his knees in front of Bam Bam.

There were two gunmen left. They had been hiding under the kitchen counter until the mayhem died down because they didn't want to get shot. The men thought Bam Bam was dead, but when they saw him at gunpoint it was the perfect time to put in work since everyone else was dead.

"Life's a bitch, ock, and you chose the wrong side," Bam Bam said, smiling.

"Allah..."

Boom! Boom!

"I don't want to hear that shit," Bam Bam said.

His two goons stood next to him as if they had put in work.

"Took a break, Phili?" said Bam Bam, looking at both men.

"Nah, we was lining son up for you, Blood," Phili said before a bullet lodged in his head along with the heads of the other gunmen before Bam Bam walked out of the back alone, the last man standing.

***

Cancun USP, PA

Marcus, a.k.a. Twin, sat in his cell. The jail was on a three month lockdown because a race riot happened on the yard. The other day a lot of good men lost their lives as the riot jumped off in the yard with the whites and Mexicans against the blacks over six dollars in stamps someone owed a D.C. cat.

The C.O. slid a paper under his door at mail time. It was the government replying to his appeal. His celly was his co-defendant, who took sixty years on a cop-out, while Marcus went to trial and got a life sentence in federal prison.

The feds was a lot different than the state because you had to run with your state, gang, or religion if you was true to it. Marcus and Sack were both on Blood time. They were the shot callers on the compound.

"Whats popping, Blood? What's that?" Sack asked, looking down from his top bunk at his celly on the bottom, who was reading something.

"I just won my appeal, Blood! I go back to court soon," he said, shocked. But he had the best lawyer in Jersey, thanks to Naya. They shared the same lawyers.

"Damn, Blood, word is bond. That's Brazy," Sack said, smiling, hoping for some play soon also.

"Facts. I touch down in them streets, I'm do all the bitches dirty who blocked my calls. I'm going hold you down, bro. Bitches going to be bringing that pack up here, watch," he stated.

"I hear you, Blood," Sack said, already used to hearing this from other inmates who went home.

Marcus had big plans to regain his turf and take over the city, but first he had to kill his brother's murderer. Word was Muhammad did it and he planned to pay him a visit. When his brother passed, he was sick and his life went downhill. He missed his twin every day.

Chapter 27
Masvingo, South Africa

A large group of African men stood around in the jungle watching a family of five burn in a small campfire. The disposed family had their bodies chopped up and eyeballs snatched out, which was a tradition in Masvingo when killing someone from either tribe.

There was a large house in the open field. African elephants slowly walked around the area, looking for food to eat. The house was heavily guarded by men with swords and bows, ready for other tribes or other wild animals like hyenas, tigers, lions, and African wild dogs.

Inside lived King Omen and his brother Zebemen. The house was decorated with dead animals, swords, fur rugs, and a collection of eyeballs and private parts in glasses on shelves.

Once the men were done with what they were doing, Zebemen led them into the house so they could clean up downstairs while he went upstairs to holla at his brother.

He knocked on his brother's wooden double doors and entered to see it dark with candles and his brother sitting Indian style in the middle of the floor praying to his devil gods as his tribe did. They worshipped devils.

"Brother, one of our men told me he has the whereabouts of your daughter Zeema, my niece. She is in the United States, in New York," Zebemen stated as his brother placed a robe made of lion fur, covering his scarred body.

Omen stood up with a poison curly snake around his neck. He loved snakes. He thought they brought humans closer to the devils.

"Bring her to me dead or alive. It's time she comes back home. I'm sure Za'alya will be delighted," Omen said in his deep African voice.

Zebemen nodded and walked towards the door, leaving his brother's room

"When you get back, send a message to our friend to let him know we're on our way," Zebemen told his men.

***

Dear, Delaware

Since Muhammad lost four of his kids already and a wife he felt lost, stressed, and nervous. He had misjudged PYT character. The bitch was official and crazy. When he hit once, she hit three times harder.

Moving his two other toddlers and wife out of town was his only move, especially after he heard the news of twenty-one people being killed in a Harlem mosque - the mosque he owned.

Not only did his Muslim brothers and sisters suffer, but his niece was killed at the young age of eight years old. He knew Bam Bam was behind the attack because of the studio shooting. The mosque killings had been on the headline news for two days, saying it was a hate crime.

He wished Malik was there because he was the most trained Muslim in his camp. He was thinking about calling Jalee and Malik so they could come to Delaware to have a talk about a new plan to take PYT out of the picture.

"Come in," Muhammad said when he heard a knock at his bedroom door. He sat at his computer, wondering if it was his guards, because his wife never knocked.

"As-salaam-alaikum," Ai Hosayni said as she stepped into the room with her hijab hiding her beautiful face. She was from Tadmur, Syria. She was Arabian and Indonesian. She spoke Arabic, Bahosa, Arancuc, and Circassion. She looked Spanish: short, curvy, long eyelashes, green eyes, long hair that was to her ass. She was twenty years old and an ex-sex slave until Muhammad bought her in Paris years ago and trained her to be an official killer. At the age of eighteen, she was very sexy. Little did he know at that time she was a born killer. Her Syria family trained her well until a terrorist group, who had better-trained killers, murdered her family and kidnapped her, then sold her into the sex trade business in Europe.

"How can I help you?" he asked her as she kept her gaze low. As a Muslim woman, this was a part of her deen.

132

"I want to help and I have an idea, Imam. I've done a little research, and I believe I can help," she said.

Muhammad sat back and listened, thinking it was time he used his wild card.

***

Bronx, NY

Cherry and Murder had just come back from a comedy show in the city.

"That shit was so fucking funny! I never been to one of those," Cherry said, driving the all-black Range through the Bronx streets.

"Yeah, that was light, babe, and you was the main sho. Everybody was on your line," he said, rolling a blunt.

"Thanks, daddy, but it's all for you," she said. She rocked a Celine mini dress with her ass busting out and Fendi red bottom heels.

"I know", he said as she stopped at a red light, rubbing his dick, ready to suck something off.

Since the beef, Murder rolled with four goons everywhere, but since Red Hat was out of town on business again, he rolled solo. He had bought Cherry her store and it was starting to get a little name for itself due to the good location in a shopping center on Gunhill Road off Boston Road.

"You need a vacation after you come back from Texas, daddy. You move around too much. Let's go the DR, babe," Cherry said as they pulled into their complex's parking lot.

Once inside, the two rushed into the bedroom and stripping naked. Within seconds, Cherry had her legs wide open as he entered her wet ocean

"Uhhhh, awwww," she moaned as his dick went in and out of her tight walls. She gave in, and ten minutes later, he felt he was about to bust, so he pulled out.

Cherry started to suck his dick. She bopped her head up and down until he nutted in her throat while twisting her head on the tip of his dick and sucking him dry.

"Damn, babe," he said, bending her over on her knees as she arched her back. He started to pound her out until she yelled his name while climaxing, making the neighbors bang on the wall.

She felt him so deep in her back that he almost fucked up some discs in her lower back until he nutted inside of her warm creamy wet pussy.

"Damn, baby, I love you," she said, out of breath, ready to grab his dick to suck it again.

"Wait a second. I'ma get some water. That Cali bud got me with the cotton mouth," he said, climbing off the bed naked in the dark room, almost slipping on her panties

"Damn, nigga, don't fall, babe," Cherry said, laughing, knowing her pussy was top notch.

Bloc, Bloc, Bloc!

Cherry received three shots to her breasts, killing her. Murder tried to grab his pistol from the floor, but it was too late. Hosayni gave him a head shot.

She made sure both of them were dead before she walked out smiling to her car, which was waiting a block away for her.

This was a test from Muhammad to see if she was ready, Hosayni had stalked them half the day. She was waiting in the closet for them. She could have been killed them, but she was fingering her small little hairy pussy to the freak show. She loved the way he fucked Cherry. It had her extra horny. She had a freaky side she couldn't control.

Chapter 28
Santiago de Cuba, Cuba

Jumbo's wife Hagor called Rugar at four in the morning, crying and sobbing on the phone informing, him Jumbo died in his sleep. Rugar was across town in the other mansion. He wasted no time heading to the main house.

Once in the house, everybody was there with sad faces, even the mayor of Cuba, along with Savannah, maids, guards, and doctors.

"I'm very sorry for the loss, Hagor. Your husband was a great, honorable man," the mayor said, standing in the living room.

"Thank you, Mayor, for coming by," Hagor stated as she walked him to the front door

"We tried to prolong his treatment so he would live longer, but he was a tough guy," Dr. Miller stated.

"I understand, Doc. Thank you for your time and help. Have a safe trip back to the States," she said.

"Okay, take care," the white doctor said as he turned around to leave, only to catch two bullets to the back of his head.

"Next time," Hagor said with a smoking gun as his blood soaked her Aubusson white rug.

Savannah sat on the couch laughing because when her mom got mad, she'd kill anybody and forget about it when she was happy again. Rugar just sat there trying to gather his thoughts. Hagor walked upstairs in her Saint Laurent silk rope in heels to go get herself together.

The maids dragged the body out of the living room while Ms. Valentia cleaned the carpet. She was a hardworking women who had been a part of the family for over twenty-five years.

"Ms. Valentia, you should take off I'll take care of this" Rugar told her taking the bucket out of her hand fill of bleach water

"Savannah, enviale rewerdos de mi porte aso madre (sends my regards to your mother)" she said as walked out the back.

"Savannah please take care of Hagor's mess while I make some calls," Rugar told her.

She just sat on the couch with her knees up, showing a little ass cheek out of her boy shorts on purpose.

"Why not? I have nothing better to do," she said with an attitude. She was still upset about the night he was giving Katie and Costilla too much attention.

"I'm sure you do have better things to do, like send your goons out to fuck up my evening only to get fucked up in return," he said, walking off with a chuckle.

Savannah's mind started to race. What if the cartels found out she was behind the hit of two powerful cartel members? She would be a dead bitch walking. She hoped Rugar kept what he knew as a secret, but how did he know all that? Now with Jumbo dead, she wondered how shit would be. She never really cared for him. All she wanted was Rugar. She could smell him miles away and every time she saw him, her pussy got wet. She had it bad. She thought about him as she scrubbed the blood off the rug.

***

Days later

The funeral was held in the brick mansion in the backyard, as Jumbo had requested before he passed. His parents were buried back there as well.

Today was the nicest day of the summer: sunny, windy, and at 97 degrees, everybody wore comfortable outfits. The backyard was packed. Every cartel family came to show their respect to the don, and the same priest who did their wedding did the funeral ceremony.

"Baby, this is crazy! Over four hundred people are here," PYT said, looking around as the priest finished his two hour speech.

"I know. Thanks for coming out on the jet on such short notice, love. I need you here right now," he said.

"Of course, why wouldn't I? And that G5 plane was popping," she said as they stood to greet the guests.

"Jasmine, thanks for coming, you look beautiful," Hagor said as she looked at PYT's Marc Jacob all-black slit dress with her six inch heels on, showing a little leg while her long hair was in a bun. "Thank you, Hagor, you looking amazing also," she said, looking at her black Gucci dress. It was classy and showing a little breast. "I'm sorry about your perdida (loss)," PYT stated.

"I'm sure I'll be okay," she replied as Savannah walked up.

"Hello, Savannah, how are you holding up?" PYT asked, not really caring how she felt. There was something about her that rubbed her the wrong way.

"Soy bueno (I'm good)," she said flatly in Spanish, wearing a tight black Hermes cropped top dress, showing her cut-up abs.

"Reading my letter at the end of the ceremony was the hardest part. But let's go do his will so I can start this big meal with the maids for our guests," Hagor said, walking inside the mansion as all the guest flooded the house talking, drinking and reminiscing.

***

In Jumbo's private office it was Hagor, PYT, Rugar, and Savannah.

"This is all he left. I'ma read it," Hagor said as she picked up a letter from Jumbo.

"I'm dead now. Please live your life. I lived mines, as my young'uns in New York say. That's a fact. I would like to thank my wife for staying by my side all these years. It's crazy. She was sent to kill me, and instead fell in love with me. I was blessed to have a woman of your status by my side. I'm blessed to have Jamel, a.k.a. Rugar, as a nephew. You're a true gentleman. Keep our bloodline flowing, please. As for your wife, watch out! You got you a real one. Don't take her lightly or for granted. She is a different breed. I'm sure she is with you now. You're a lucky man. To Savannah, I wish you luck in life. You have a lot to learn. To my maids, thank you. I have a million dollars for each of my maids. To Rugar, I leave my big mansion and the rest of my homes. Hagor can divide as she pleases. Each of you have an offshore account with a billion dollars - except you, Savannah. Thanks to PYT, we did this months ago. Love you all."

Savannah's face was beet red as she got up and ran out of the room slamming the door

"She will be okay. It's not about her anymore, plus she don't even know the value of a dollar," Hagor said, placing the letter in her pocket.

"Wow! I can't believe this! It all feels as if it happened so fast," Rugar said.

"Yeah, so enjoy life while you can. I'ma go help cook for the guests. Thanks for being here. Jumbo really cared for you both, and that's rare," Hagor said, walking out.

"I'ma go help cook. I love you," PYT said, leaving him alone in his uncle's office to think and get his plans and emotions together.

Chapter 29
Brooklyn

Bam Bam and his goons had just walked out of Club Nasty.

"You saw how shawty was popping that shit on the pole, Blood?" one of the goons said while walking into the club parking lot.

"I tried to pay shawty a band for some pussy, skrap, but she was acting bougie with her pussy smelling like up north mackerel in a can," Big Dot said, throwing shade. He was really upset the thick, dark-skinned bitch wouldn't give him no ass.

"Her shit trash, Blood. She from my hood. But her head game is brazy, homie," Rosaza stated, climbing in a Hummer truck on big rims.

"Ay yo, Big Dot, you and S. Dot roll with me to the hotel because I need y'all to handle it. They supposed to drop it off in an hour," Bam Bam as he climbed in the driver seat of his Benz truck, playing a Jadakiss album.

One truck followed Bam Bam and the other two trucks went the opposite direction to handle some business. Last month the Feds did a sweep, snatching sixty-five of his men off the streets. The Muslims were making Brooklyn hot to the point where NYPD was hopping out and begging niggas to stop the killing at least on their shift.

Bam Bam rode through the mean violent Brooklyn streets with a Draco in his lap, thinking about a Spanish woman named Candy he met at a designer clothing shop on Fifth Avenue two weeks ago.

He saw Candy and had to have her. She was beautiful: colorful eyes, slim, beautiful. She had her own crib, car, and she was single. The two been texting back and forth for days and tonight was the night they planned to have a chill date at a hotel.

Bam Bam wanted her to come to his condo, but she refused, so they both agreed on a public place like a hotel.

She had been texting him while he was in the club, letting him know she was getting horny, letting him know tonight he was getting out of the friend zone.

***

Once in Downtown Brooklyn, he pulled up to a nice hotel with a waterfall out front, glass windows, marble floors, and expensive paintings on the walls.

"Y'all can wait or come back in a couple of hours, Blood. I'ma be a while," Bam Bam said as he parked in the rear lot.

"A'ight, we got you, bro. As soon as we get back from picking up the shipment across town," Big Dot said, pulling off as Bam Bam walked in the hotel.

She texted him the sixth floor room number and he made his way to the elevator with a hard-on already.

The door was open as he entered. As soon as he saw the dim lights, he walked past the kitchen to see her standing in the middle of the living room floor.

Candy wore a one piece G-string covering her small breasts and her small pussy, leaving a side lip out.

"You made it, papi," she said, hugging him as he looked at her fit, toned body. He could tell she worked out.

"Me too," he said as she led him into the back master bedroom, grabbing his hand.

"You smell good. I wonder how you taste," he said as they entered a dim room. She sat on the bed, legs wide out

"Taste it now," she said as she moved the G-string to the side, showing her small pink clit between her perfect lips.

Bam Bam started sucking on her pussy, making her squirm and shake. He ate her out until she squirted because she was a squirter, which he loved.

After she came, Candy told him she wanted to tie him up and suck his dick and ride him while he fucked her ass. He quickly agreed as she placed real cuffs on him.

"Damn, these shit lock and all," he said as she smiled at him.

He had no clue the little good girl was such a big freak. He loved this type of shit.

"When you done, I want you to finger my ass and stick that broomstick in me while I jerk off. I got a freaky side too," Bam Bam said as Candy looked shocked. When she took off his Gucci pants, she saw that he wore a large pair of pink panties with a three-inch dick curled up.

"Damn," she whispered, rubbing it, having never seen a dick so small.

"Huh?"

"Nothing, daddy," she said, sucking his dick until it got hard one extra inch.

"I'ma give you a night to remember," she said, placing a blindfold over him

"I bet, you nasty little bitch! I want to taste your piss and shit!" he shouted as her stomach turned.

Bam Bam was a bio-sexual thug. Nobody knew about this lifestyle except his wife, who had recently divorced him. If anybody was to ever find out about this, he would have been labeled a homo thug and kicked out of the Blood and the Empire, but his heart was a disease.

Candy's real name was Al Hosayhi. She was grossed out by this fat muthafucka, she couldn't wait to wash her body off and her mouth out. She got dressed quickly in an all-black garment and hijab as she came inside the hotel.

"Damn, ma, you about to get my dick limp," he said.

"I got you, love. I'ma make it worth it," she moaned, placing a ball in his mouth and strapping duct tape around his mouth to hold it in place as he moaned.

"Hmmmm." He was moaning loud.

"Shhhhh," she said, untying his blindfold. He had never had sex with a bitch dressed up like a Muslim. He looked at her oddly, thinking it was her fantasy maybe.

"You ready for the surprise?" she said, pulling out a long sharp blade as her accent changed from Spanish to Arabian.

Bam Bam's eyes widened. He knew this was no game now. He realized it was a set up and he couldn't move an inch because he was cuffed and tied to the bed frame.

"I'm Hosayni, and today I will let your blood honor the death of my brothers and sisters you killed," she said, stabbing him thirty times, slicing his neck open and leaving him dead.

She'd been tracking him for weeks, so when she followed him to Fifth Avenue to go shopping, she knew it would be the perfect time to approach him. It was so easy.

They texted all day for weeks so she figured tonight would be perfect and it was. She had to change her accent and name are he would have caught on Muhammad told her. She left the hotel smiling, knowing the Iman would be proud of her.

Chapter 30
Newark, NJ

The cool breeze blew through PYT's long straight hair as she sat in MLK City Park on the old bench, watching the ducks chase each other. The more she watched the ducks chase and fight each other for crumbs the more they reminded her of people.

The last couple of months had been rough on her, but she was still standing stronger than ever/ Bullet and Big Smokey on the west coast networking and trying to open shop was a good look for the Empire.

Bam Bam's death struck everyone's heart. He was one of the most loved men in the city of Brooklyn besides Black Knowledge from East New York and OG Chuck from the Stuy. Regardless, his seat in the Empire had to be replaced soon, and that was why she was here today.

PYT spoke to Naya and they both thought Twin would be a perfect fit for the Empire. Now with him home off his appeal, he was already taking over the city.

The murder rate was at an all-time high in the city of Newark with the Crips, Muslims, and Bloods since Twin touched down last month.

The night Bam Bam was found murdered, nobody knew anything except that he was seeing a Spanish woman who was nowhere in sight when his body was found the next morning by room service.

PYT knew it was an inside job because the killer stole all of his personal belongings expect the pink panties he had on while being chained to the hotel bed.

"Where the fuck is he at?" she mumbled to herself, waiting for Twin to arrive at their set location. It was 8 a.m., so nobody was really out except white people walking their dogs and Spanish men chilling.

"'Bout fucking time," she said as two BMW trucks pulled up back to back outside the park.

Twin bopped through the park with his dreads swinging and covering his face, in his all-red Gucci Sweatsuit.

"What's goody? Long time, no see," he said, hugging her lightly. The two used to kick it daily when she used to come out to Jersey to chill with Naya.

"Likewise. Glad you home, bro. I hear you out here going crazy," she said.

"Yeah, niggas thought it was over, but I always kept faith in Allah. If it wasn't for Naya, I wouldn't be here. I been hearing a lot word in the streets that Rugar is alive. That's brazy," Twin said, sitting down, looking around to see a couple of Spanish niggas sitting and walking around talking. But he knew something was off about them.

"They're with me; it's cool. But let me get to the real reason why I called you out here. For one, you're an official stand up nigga, Blood, and I respect that you could have easily told to get a time cut or your case dropped, but you held it down. Then the power you have out here alone is very useful when it comes to getting this money. I run the Empire now and I'm also a lead member of the Cartel as well as Rugar. A lot changed in the past three years," she said.

"Damn, my nigga," he said, shocked

"We lost Bam Bam, and I want you to take his seat within the Empire. You deserve it. I think it's only right, Blood. We a family under the Omerta law and we control the East Coast drug trade, and Jersey will be all yours, bro. We already voted you in. Your name and loyalty holds it on weight," she said as she looked at his mute facial expression.

"I'm down. Say less. When do I start?" he stated, knowing it was the right move because Brazy and Naya basically raised him and his brother, whom Muhammad had murdered years ago.

"Welcome to the family, Blood, and no worries about Muhammad. We are one step away from finding him. Trust me, he will be out of hiding soon. He's too money hungry," she said, knowing he was heavy on his mind, because he was heavy on hers.

144

***

Cuba

Hagor got up from her bed to go get some tissue from her private bathroom. Her ass cheeks hung out the bottom of her booty shorts.

Rugar and Hagor were in her room talking about Jumbo and the good times they shared with him. She went to wipe her tears when she thought about their first Honeymoon in Cihiayi, Taiwan. The honeymoon was special. They learned about the Taoist religion on Kueishonato Island which was Taiwan's only historically active volcano.

"I can't believe this," she said, sitting back down, looking a Rugar sitting on the edge of her bed trying to be supportive during the hard times. Out of nowhere, Hagor kissed his lips. He wanted to move back, but he couldn't.

They both kissed passionately while climbing in the bed, the same bed Hagor and Jumbo slept in. She got undressed and undressed him while both of their hormones were to the max.

Hagor saw his hard massive dick and began sucking it slowly with her thick wet lips. His dick was disappearing into her throat so fast he had to tell her to slow down before he came.

She made her way down to his balls as pre-cum slowly leaked out the tip. She sucked his balls while jerking his dick. Then she bopped up and down on the head, slurping it like an icy cone.

When she was done, he laid her down and ate her out clean. She had a nice pussy with tan lips, but it was phat like a mitten, nicely shaved.

"Ohhh, uhhhh," she moaned she climaxed in his face. She never had her pussy eaten like that. Her pussy lips were swollen like black eyes.

Rugar lifted her right leg over his shoulder and slid his hard dick into her soaked pussy as she moaned, jumping back. Rugar dug deep into her tight, warm pussy that was extra creamy.

"Papi, yesss, oh my God, papi," she said as he slowly long-stroked, touching the deep bottom walls.

145

He came in her. When he slid his dick out, cum was pouring out of her pussy like water as she rubbed her clit, cumming.

She laid him down and wiggled her ass on his dick. He slowly slid in and out of her wetness while sucking her nipples. Hagor bounced her ass up and down on his dick until she came hard, which made her body shiver.

"Fuck, you got some good pussy! Bend over," he said, feeling the animal come out as she bent over to reveal a wide large ass. He entered her from behind and pounded her back out while spreading her ass cheeks, filling her up with dick, making her go crazy

"Uhhhh, umm, I can't take it!" she cried as her titties bounced back and forth. She slammed into his dick for fifteen minutes straight.

"Ya vay espare un minuto, papi!" she yelled, saying she was cumming again. She was tired and weak as he busted on her ass.

Rugar slapped her ass roughly three times, leaving a red mark on her ass as he slid in and out of her pussy until he came.

Rugar was sweating, but he couldn't stop. Her pussy had control over him already. Rugar saw she was worn out, but Rugar's blood pressure was pumping. He bent her over the bed to see her phat pretty pussy lips wide open. She began playing with it while licking her lips.

Rugar grabbed her waist as he slid in her from behind. She started to throw it back wildly while making it clap on his thighs. Rugar was surprised at how big her ass was. He almost lost balance as he came. Hagor came at the same time while grabbing the pillow for dear life. He pounded her from the back as the headboard banged on the wall.

Once they were done, they were exhausted. They both were freaks and as they sat there, they started to think about what just happened. They agreed it would never happen again and went separate ways, each feeling like a different person.

But little did they know somebody had heard and seen every second of their affair.

Chapter 31
Miami, FL

Muhammad had just arrived in Miami from Delaware to meet with his connect. He was dressed in a women's disguise, wearing a sundress, wig, makeup, heels, and extra lip gloss. Lately he had been hiding, trying to figure out his next move, because he was losing a lot of good men in the process.

Once outside Miami International, there was a 6'8" 305 pound black gorilla nigga standing next to a Porsche limo.

"Good morning, how may I help you?" the big man asked as he saw Muhammad approaching dressed as a woman. He thought he was an ugly bitch with wide shoulders.

"I'm Muhammad. I'm here for Ronell. I just dress like this as a disguise," Muhammad stated.

The guard looked at him as if he was crazy. He leaned in the car to tell to his boss.

"Ike, pat that bitch down and make sure you grab his dick," Ronell said seriously as Big Ike frowned.

"I gotta pat you down," Big Ike said.

Muhammad lifted his arms as Ike began patting him down. As soon as he got between his legs, he hit his dick and balls as if it was an accident.

"Owwweee, man, what the fuck is wrong with you?" Muhammad shouted as if he was ready to fight.

"Sorry about that, sir. Protocol," Big Ike stated. He opened the door while sweat poured down his forehead from the Miami heat.

"Protocol my ass! Next time you won't be so lucky," Muhammad said as he rubbed his smooth clean face, missing his big beard as he climbed in the limo.

"Mr. Muhammad, nice to finally meet you. I've heard a lot of good about you. I hope your trip was pleasant. I'm sure you and my security guard Ike got well acquainted already," Ronell said with a chuckle as he saw Big Ike look at Muhammad and put his head down.

"Seems to me this trip been due for a long time. Thank you for having me," he replied as the limo sped down the highway.

"I'ma let you get settled in the Four Seasons hotel, then we will have a dinner at my mansion. I have plans to take you to a couple of clubs after we discuss business in private," Ronell said driving down Collins Avenue.

***

Hours later

At dinner, Muhammad was dressed in his black garment and black Kufi. Malik just called him and told him he was going to Delaware to check on his wife. Muhammad stepped out of the limo in front of a large mansion made of glass with blue lights all around it. There were seven luxury cars parked throughout the long narrow drive-way everything from Benz, Lambo's, Jaguar, Maybachs, a new two tone white and gray Wraith.

He was escorted into the mansion by three guards and one of them was Ike. He tried his best to refrain from any eye contact while walking him towards the backyard where his boss awaited him.

The back had a large tent with dinner, long tables, chairs, a bar, and a grill near the pool with the crystal clear water.

Muhammad saw all the halal food as he walked up to Ronell.

"Good evening Mr. Muhammad. I ordered you the best halal food in the city. I try my best to please my guests, especially a guest of business." Ronell wore a Bottega Veneta suit and Audemar Peugeot Royal watch that had cost $545,000.

"Thank you" Muhammad said, sitting down.

"Listen, we've been doing business for years and you always play fair, so that's one reason why I called you out here today. I have a new project I'm sure you will be interested in: pure cocoa leaves transformed into pills. 100 pills is 1008 grams a brick. My connect and I are negotiating a price now. She is speaking to her people as we speak," Ronell said smoothly.

Muhammad was in deep thought. He wondered how many times he could step on one pill.

"Okay, cool, I'm down. How much will I need to start off with, you think?" Muhammad said.

"Give me a week to figure everything out, then we're good to go. I just wanted to make sure you're aboard," Ronell said.

"Say no more. We locked in then," Muhammad said, smiling, knowing he was about to see a gold mine.

"How's the east coast? There is a lot of drama up there I see daily on the news," Ronell said, shaking his head.

"Things slowed down a little since I fell back from the scenes and let my sons run the show," he said.

"I wish I could help. I got some people I can reach out to," he said, hoping to help his client so he would be able to focus more on money than violence.

"These people are a different type of breed. They call themselves the Empire. A chick runs it named PYT. This bitch is poison. She killed my family. I will do everything in my power to kill her whole bloodline," Muhammad said, getting mad at the thought of her.

Ronell was silent as his brain started to quickly piece everything together.

"I'ma make a quick call to solve all your problems. Give me one second," Ronell said, excusing himself from the table.

Ten minutes later, he walked back outside with an iPhone in his hand as she sat down

"Everything is taken care of, my friend," Ronell said.

"Damn, that was fucking fast! How did you do it? I've been trying for months. Thank you," said Muhammad.

"Not so fast, bruh-bruh," Ronell said, placing a pistol on the table. "PYT is Naya's sister, and Naya is my wife," Ronell said as Muhammad choked on his water.

Ronell didn't even give him a chance to speak. He emptied the clip into his face and walked back in the house to call Naya back, because she was waiting on his call. Ten minutes ago, he asked her if she knew a Muhammad from Jersey who was getting money and beefing with PYT, and she confirmed it.

Big Ike and his men cleaned up the body and placed Muhammad in a garbage bag. Then they took his body to the closest river so he could swim with the fish.

Chapter 32
Dear, Delaware

PYT brought Twin along with her on her mission only because he knew the Delaware area. She hated driving through Delaware's country roads with a speed limit of 35 mph.

They were parked on a small dirt road which was a long drive way leading to the two story yellow house sitting up the road on the small land full of trees, high uncut grass, and a barn on the side of the house. As well as six guards surrounding the house.

Nobody would ever think a drug lord would be hiding out somewhere like this. There were no street lights, so the area was extremely dark. PYT came prepared, dressed in all-black with night vision googles, rifles, and a vest.

"I don't think he here, sis. That nigga scared of his own shadow" Twin said looking into the house windows with the googles to see a light skin women praying with two small children.

"That could have been him in one of those trucks that left twenty minutes," she said, lying to herself because she had seen a gang of young niggas hop in the truck, and one of them was Young Malik.

"Nah, Blood, them was young niggas. But what you trying to do? We been sitting in this van all day. If we going in, let's go, but first we got to get past these niggas," Twin said, pointing at the six niggas posted up around the house.

"Time to eat," she said, grabbing her AR-7 assault rifle hoping out of the van, tiptoeing in the darkest area of the path leading to the house.

***

Muhammad's second wife, Lipa, had just got done making the night prayer with the kids. She was now waiting on Young Malik to come back with some fast food for them so they could go to sleep.

Lipa was a thirty-six-year-old with light skin, a pretty thin frail woman from Philly. She had been married to Muhammad for ten years. Her son was six and their daughter was eight. Her life was strictly around her Islamic religion and her children. Lipa was well-trained. She had trained Young Malik and most of Muhammad's army. She was a licensed martial arts teacher.

"I'ma ask Muhammad if we can move to Arizona, sis. I'm sure the kids would love that instead of being trapped in the woods with all these deer and mountain lions" she told her sister on the phone.

"Okay. I'ma call you tomorrow. Let me go check on these kids I know they starving. As-salaam-alaikum," Lipa said as she got up from the couch.

"Slow down," Twin said, standing directly behind her with a Tommy gun to see a scared look on her face.

PYT walked in the house slowly. She had an oversize special made silencer on her AR-7 so it wouldn't alert her visitors.

"How did you two get in and what do you——"

"Bitch, shut up! Where the fuck is Muhammad? I ask all the questions!" she shouted, cutting Lipa off.

"What and who are you talking about? You have the wrong home. Please leave before I call the police," Lipa stated knowing there was no way she could beat the two gunmen with their assault rifles

"Okay, let's play," PYT said as she ran upstairs and came back down with her son and daughter crying. PYT led them into the living room.

"Mommy!" her cute daughter said as PYT kicked both of them in their asses, making them fly to the floor.

"Now once again, where is he?" PYT asked, pointing her AR at the kid.

"I don't know! Please, not them!" Lipa cried.

"Five, four, three, two..."

"Please, I don't know!"

"One."

The little girl's head exploded all over the back of the couch.

"Oh nooo, nooo!" Lipa yelled out.

"She not playing, lady, you better give her something," Twin said, holding her at gunpoint.

"I'ma fucking kill you, bitch, I swear to Allah!" Lipa shouted as tears rolled down her smooth face

"I heard it all, but it's obvious you not going to give him up, so we out," PYT said, shooting her in her upper torso and face while Twin shot the little boy who had never shed a tear the whole time.

The two left the trail of bodies as they climbed in the van, hopping back on the highway

"There goes the rest of them," Twin said as two trucks drove past them on the highway, paying them no mind.

"Let them deliver the message," PYT said with a laugh, wondering where Muhammad could be.

***

New York

Rugar was home with his wife. The two had fucked for about two hours and now he was out cold and snoring. PYT felt there was something extremely off about him with his sex, vibe, swag, and energy. His sex drive was never low and as a woman, she could feel when her lover was cheating. Normally her pussy would be sore right now, but she didn't even climax tonight. She was pissed.

She had just come from checking on Lil Brazy. It was one in the morning and she couldn't sleep. She was reading *Murda Season Part 1* in her bed, thinking about Rugar and China's upcoming birthday. She wanted to plan something special for them both.

Out of nowhere, she heard Rugar talking in his sleep, something he never did. She stopped reading and paid close attention because growing up, her mother always told her 90% of what a person says in their sleep talk is true.

"Ummm, stop, no! Damn Hagor, suck that dick again! Your pussy good. Ride it. Ummm," Rugar moaned.

PYT had tears in her eyes.

She pulled out a long blade from under her pillow and looked at him, ready to slit his throat. Her gut feeling was right. He was cheating. The more she looked at him, the more she wait wanted to kill him.

She got dressed and wrote him a note, telling him she was going out of town, and left the house.

***

Cuba

The next day, PYT walked into the mansion where Hagor lived to see nobody there, which was perfect. She wore an army camouflage outfit with her hair in a Chinese bun. She set her bookbag down in the living room, walking through the house.

As soon as she entered the kitchen, she saw Hagor sitting on a stool, drinking coffee and watching a Spanish soap opera. She wore black leggings and a green Nike tank top that held her perky, firm breasts in place. She was about to begin her morning exercise.

"PYT, to what do I owe this visit to?" Hagor asked, not even looking in her direction. Hagor had a feeling Jasmine would one day arrive at her home upset because she had found out about hers and Rugar's affair.

"I'm sure a hoe as yourself should know why I'm here," PYT said, sitting down next to her, taking her cup of coffee and drinking it. Neither woman showed any type of fear.

"I'm surprised he told you so fast. But it's not what you think, Jasmine. Woman to woman, it was a one-time thing. I was lonely, sad, and depressed. He was the only one here. To be real, if Bill Cosby was here, I most likely would have fucked him and sucked his dick," Hagor said, being honest.

"He didn't tell me shit. But you just slept with your dead husband's nephew. You're fucking nasty! You picked the wrong dick. I hope it was worth dying for," she said, standing up.

"It was good enough to die for twice," she said, standing up now face to face with PYT. "Follow me," Hagor said, walking downstairs into a large room with a blue mat covering the floor, exercise equipment, swords on the walls, guns, and all types of foreign weapons.

***

"I'm a fair woman, Jasmine...PYT...Zeema...whatever you like to be called. I have over thirty years in training to your twenty-three years on earth," Hagor stated, grabbing two medium-sized double-edged swords off the wall and tossing her one, which she caught in the air

"Twenty-four, bitch. Enough talking. Let's work," PYT said, taking off her ACG boots, now barefoot.

Both women began to circle each other while grabbing their swords tightly. Hagor attacked first, swinging her sword at PYT full force. PYT ducked every swing while backpedaling. She slowed down, getting pissed at her attempts. The young girl was swift.

PYT waited for the perfect time and hit her with a fast round house jump kick to the head, dazing Hagor. With the upper hand, PYT rushed her with her sword, swinging it side to side, up and down, and in circles.

Hagor tried to protect herself in defensive mood, but PYT cut a big piece out of her stomach and blood squirted through her green top.

"You stupid bitch!" Hagor yelled, now mad. Hagor ran toward PYT, catching her off guard, cornering her, swinging like a madwoman, stabbing PYT in the shoulder deeply.

"Uggggh, damn!" PYT said, sliding away from the corner as Hagor smiled.

"I'm too advanced for you, African Princess. I'm very sure your mother will be disappointed in you. Me and her used to be close," Hagor said, confusing her.

PYT wondered how she knew her mother because she hadn't seen her in years. She and Naya thought she was dead.

PYT had to do something quick, so she did two front flips with her sword, making Hagor back up. They went sword for sword with sparks flying in the air. PYT was able to knock Hagor's sword out of her hand, then she pushed her sword into her heart.

Blood poured out of Hagor's mouth. PYT roughly pulled her sword out of her ribcage to see Hagor's eyes fully widen with a surprised look. PYT drop kicked her body to the floor as Hagor's body laid in her puddle of blood.

"Fucking nasty old bitch! Never fuck with a bitch's husband or family," PYT said as she spit and kicked her lifeless body.

PYT realized she was short on time. Her next flight left in an hour. She had to fly back home to make it look like she was only out shopping. She snatched her Versace bookbag, called a cab, and left with a T-shirt wrapped around her fresh wound. It wasn't bleeding as much anymore, but she still had to get to an airport bathroom to clean it before she got on the flight.

She knew Hagor knew something about her mother - who she was and where she was - but now with her dead, PYT might never know. But killing Hagor was something she had to do. She refused to let any bitch fuck up her marriage or happy life.

Chapter 33
Miami, FL

"She looks so amazing. I'm proud of her," PYT told Rugar as they sat in the audience with other families, watching their loved ones walk across the stage to get their college degrees from the University of Miami.

"Me too. Time flies. I remember she was going to give all of this up because her boyfriend got killed," Rugar said as China walked across the stage, smiling from ear to ear.

"I can get her a position with my firm if she is willing to go through the process. I believe she will be a great candidate," PYT said as the crowd yelled and shouted for their loved ones.

"If that's what she wants. You know she got her own life down here: friends, boyfriend, a job now, car, a crib she loves," he stated

Today was sunny, warm, and the perfect day for a ceremony in the back of the college on the football field. After the students gave their speeches, it was over for most of them while some of them planned to work on their Master's and Ph.D.

"Brother! Oh my God, you made it!" China said happily.

"I'm proud of you," he said, hugging her.

"You did good. You deserve it," PYT said giving her a light hug as China admired her off-white yellow dress with the back cropped out.

Seconds later, Pressure and Ronell approached the three. Both men wore suits, looking like businessmen instead of gangstas.

"Congratulations, baby," Pressure said, hugging her, lifting her in the air, spinning her like a doll.

"Rugar, nice to meet you again," Pressure said, shaking his hand and introducing himself to PYT respectfully.

"You did very well, China. The hard work paid off," Ronell said, looking at her guest.

"Oh! Ronell, this is my brother Rugar and his wife PYT," she said, smiling. All her friends and family were there.

"Nice to meet the both of you finally," Ronell said, extending his hand to them

"Nice to meet you, brother-in-law. Naya told us so much about you your family," PYT said as Rugar nodded his head in agreement.

"It's a blessing from Allah to finally meet you both. But can I have a second from the both of you in private? China and Pressure, hold steady," Ronell said, walking through the crowds of people until Rugar, PYT, and him were away from civilians.

"Glad to have the both of you here. I've been waiting to link up. But as you know, we all have busy lifestyles. I feel as if we're already family, thanks to my wife she speaks so highly of you both and you know that's rare," Ronell said, laughing.

PYT couldn't lie. Her sister had found a winner. Ronell was sexy as fuck and he was respectful. Even Rugar liked him.

"I heard a lot about you down here. I respect your movement, son," Rugar said.

"Thanks, likewise. But there is something I want to bring up that crossed my attention. My wife told me y'all was having issues with the Muslims up top, and it just so happens I found out may main east coast client was Muhammad."

When Ronell said this, PYT and Rugar looked at each other.

"After a dinner meeting with him, he mentioned he was having problems with a woman named PYT, so I called Naya and asked her if that was the Muslim dude she was talking about from Jersey and she said yeah," Ronell stated.

"Where is he?" PYT asked, ready to kill.

"He's dead. I killed him days ago," Ronell said as if it was nothing.

PYT heard Muhammad had a powerful connect after the Africans cut him off, but she had no clue it was Ronell, her sister's husband.

"Thank you. We can repay——"

"Never. You're family," he told Rugar.

"Take our private number. My sister is my life. I know she is in good hands. But you can still always reach out," Rugar told him, handing him a piece of paper.

"Okay. I have a meeting in Houston so I have to go, but I want y'all to go to my club tomorrow for China's birthday bash. And happy birthday to you too, Rugar Enjoy the city," Ronell said, walking off to his four linebacker security guards.

"I knew something was wrong, I wanted to kill that nigga myself," she said as they walked back towards China.

"It's over now. Just regain his turf," Rugar said.

"Who is this, China?" asked Fatima when she saw Rugar and PYT walk up to them.

China didn't tell Fatima she had a brother. Fatima's pierced pussy was dripping wet down her thick thighs. Rugar was sexy and she wanted him bad.

"That's my brother Rugar and his wifey," China said, dragging out the word wifey so Fatima could get the picture and close her mouth before it got rusty.

"I got a couple of events lined up around the city at the best clubs for y'all birthday weekend," Pressure said, breaking the ice because Fatima had no clue who PYT was. But he did, and he would hate to see her lose her life just for being thirsty.

"It's getting hot. Let's get out of here," Rugar said walking to his eight guards posted near the football field bleachers.

PYT stopped China as they were walking off the field

"Your little friend needs to slow her roll before she gets rolled," PYT said seriously.

"She knows better. But fuck her. She going home. I'm trying to turn up," China said as they followed their men to the parking lot.

**

The night was partying non-stop. Everybody was tipsy. They partied until the morning hours to bring in their birthday. They all had a good time out. Pressure and Rugar got close. Pressure reminded him of Montana before he was killed.

The after party was at Pressure's mansion in Key West. But it wasn't much of an after party because everybody came back and went to sleep.

"Happy birthday. I had a good time, baby. I love you so much," PYT said laying naked in Pressure guest room listen to Rugar heart after an hour of rough crazy sex.

"I love you too, baby. I have something important to tell you, but I don't need you to overreact," Rugar said, sitting up, ready to get his affair off his chest because it'd been killing him. He hadn't seen Hagor since, but he felt it was the right time. Rugar looked into her gray soft eyes and couldn't do it at all.

"What, babe?" she asked, playing dumb.

"Nothing, boo. I love you. Let's go to sleep so we can go back home tomorrow and take Brandon out," Rugar said as he kissed her forehead. He heard his private Cuban phone going off, which had only happened once when Jumbo died from cancer.

"Hello? Hold on, I can't hear, you slow down," Rugar said, jumping out the bed. PYT heard a woman on the other end screaming her lungs out.

"Okay, I'll be there soon, calm down," he said, hanging up with a confused, stressed expression.

"What happened now?" she asked flatly.

"Someone killed Hagor in her house. They believe it was a crew of assassins. I have to get back to figure this shit out," he said, getting dressed, missing her evil expression. "I'm so sorry, babe! But when I'm done, I'll be back, or you can come," he said, sounding distressed, making her stomach flip to see him get any type of emotion about bitches, especially a bitch he fucked.

"Do you love me?" PYT asked softly.

"Of course you know I do, boo. I don't have time for your little games. I have to go," Rugar said, putting on his Tom Ford shoes about to call his G-5 jet plot and tell him to get ready.

"You may want to sit down for this. I know you had an affair with that old bitch Hagor. I heard you in your sleep dreaming about the bitch, so I went to Cuba and asked her, then I killed her. You fucking cheated on me!"

"Fuck, Jasmine! Why did you kill her? She is non-active, but she is still a respected Cartel leader. This shit can backfire. Now I got to clean this shit up."

"I'm sorry. I was mad. Don't cheat next time. I love you," she said, crying.

He apologized, kissed her, and walked out.

Chapter 34
Cuba
Cartel meeting

After two hours of talking, speeches, concerns, and worries, the families were willing to give Rugar's new pill product a try. This meeting was only held one time a year, so the families would express all of their issues.

Rugar sat at the head of the table. Today the meeting was set up under a tent in the back with a long table, chair, and a nice cool breeze. PYT sat in her seat wearing a white top, blazer, and slacks, showing her abs and flat stomach. She wore a red bra and red bottom heels.

"If I may say, your new idea is brilliant, sir. It's a gold mine," the leader of the French family stated as most of the other cartel families nodded their heads.

"Since you and your wife took over, my country has been seeing 17% more profit and I'm sure other families have seen greater profit also. We all thank you. But we need to get to the bottom of Hagor's murder. She was a very likable women and loved by many of us. I don't understand how someone of her skills can die the way she did," Juda of the Egypt Cartel said.

"Where was her security?" Razak from the Malaysia Cartel family asked.

"I agree she was an honorable woman among us. We have to find her killer. She saved my wife's life years ago before she got ill and passed," Mr. Ying Lak from the Thailand Cartel said.

"I agree, mon," Shota said. He ran the Jamaican Cartel. He looked at Katie as she rolled her eyes. She hated him.

PYT's palms started to get a little sweaty. She started to feel a little uncomfortable, but she tried her best to keep a poker face on. Costilla just so happened to look at PYT to see her forehead was sweating and she had a nervous look on her face, but she paid her no mind, thinking she was on coke.

Rugar sat there quietly, listening to their concerns about Hagor's death

"I'm well of aware of the situation that took place. Me and my wife was in Miami, but from my understanding, she gave security and all the workers a day off for Liberation Day. Her daughter Savannah was unaware of the devastation as well. I have my men on it as we-speak so this will not go unanswered," Rugar said as he stood.

"I hope so, Mr. Rugar," said Mr. Hubei from the China Cartel in Beijing. Hagor and Hubei were close friends when Hagor lived in Beijing. He taught her a lot of her kung-fu.

The meeting lasted twenty more minutes, then everyone went there ways, waiting on the new product.

***

Rugar was in his office alone, thinking about a cover up for Hagor's murder. It was easy to frame a nigga, then kill him, then move on with life.

"Babe, you forgot to say bye to everyone. I had to shake hands and hug babies. I hate that shit. But you okay?" PYT asked, sitting down with a slight worried look on her face.

"I'm straight," he said, looking at her.

"I'm sorry," she stated again, putting her head down.

"It's cool, love. It's really my fault. But I'm sure it will blow over soon. I'ma handle it. You my wife. I'll put my life on the line for you."

"I hope so, Mr. Brown, I hope so. But I have to fly back home. Brandon starts school and I have a meeting with the Empire this week," she said, standing up.

"Okay. Hopefully sometime this week the lab testers will have everything ready. I paid this scientist a lot of money to create this shit so it better be what it's supposed to be," he stated.

"It will babe, have patience. I love you. I'ma use your jet to get home," she said, walking out.

He watched her ass move side to side. "Jasmine!" he called out. He never used her real name unless he was upset.

"Yes?" She turned around.

"Next time, never let them see you sweat," he said, logging on to his computer to do some research.

***

New York City

PYT sat at the head of the round table in her black Ralph Lauren dress and six inch high heels.

"Glad we could all make it. Rugar sends his Blood love to you all. I got love for every soul in this room, not just because all of you Bloods are on go time, but because loyalty makes us family. It's loyalty before royalty," PYT said, looking around the small ballroom Bullet owned, which he used to throw parties in or let rappers, NBA, and NFL players rent out to throw events in.

"We love your crazy ass too," Big Smokey stated.

"Whatever, nigga. But first, I want everyone to embrace Twin. He can never replace Bam Bam, but he's one of us. Another person I've been looking at is Glizzy. He been moving for us in Atlanta," said PYT.

"I agree. Boy on his shit. He rock solid. I think he deserves a shot, Blood - at least one day," Red Hat stated.

"One day, I can assure you. But good news: Muhammad was murdered in Miami weeks ago, so he a dead issue," PYT said.

"How the fuck is that if I'm still having shootouts?" Red Hat said.

"Yeah, they hitting me too," Big Smokey stated.

"I think that's his son Young Malik causing all this drama, but he will come out of hiding soon as well," PYT stated strongly.

Twin was happy to hear Muhammad was dead. "Thank you for the opportunity. My heart been here since Brazy and Naya was here, but I'm just glad to be home and regaining the streets again," Twin said.

"No doubt, brotty. But PYT, what's popping with that new product?" Bullet said.

"Rugar is working on that now. It should be all good within a couple of weeks. But on some serious shit, I have a strong vibe we're going to be up against a powerful force that's going to make or break us. We need a stronger army and more gun power," she said as nobody said a word.

"Say no more. You heard we ready," Red Hat said, ready for some smoke.

Twin was about to say something until the lights shut off and shots could be heard from outside. All of them grabbed their assault rifles from under the table.

"Split up now!" PYT yelled as gunmen busted in the double doors shooting. The only light in the ballroom was from the windows.

Bullets were coming from everywhere. Everybody took cover. PYT took out three gunmen while Red Hat and Twin double teamed. They was outnumbered five to forty. They only came with an eight man security team because the ballroom was a public place next to a city hall near Times Square.

"Duck, Bullet!" yelled Big Smokey, shooting two gunmen, kicking them down and saving Bullet's life.

"Block me, Smokey," PYT said, posted up near a small stage, shooting every target.

"Come on, we out," Big Smoke said, running in the middle of the floor to help Red Hat and Twin, going round for round with their 100 round drums.

Tat-tat-tat! Bloc! Boom! Tat-tat!

PYT shot two men trying to cover a nigga who was moving fast as lighting as if he was a professional.

"Ugggh, shit, I'm hit," Twin said, taking two bullets to the side, dragging himself to the wall.

PYT was giving out all head shots - no receipts or funds back. She was clearing out the room alone.

"Fuck, I gotta get out of here!" Malik said as he saw a back door exit near the stage.

"Malik, come out to play!" PYT shouted. She saw Malik run and slide across the floor while everybody shot at him, but missed because it was too dark near the back door. There were no windows back there.

Bullet and Big Smokey took Twin out front and put him in a truck, rushing him to a hospital, while PYT ran out back looking for Malik only to see him long gone.

"Fuck!" she shouted, running back in to see one Muslim left with no gun in his hand.

"He pay for pussy at Fox Lane once a week, please!" the young man screamed, covering his face, hoping she spared his life. He was a school kid trying to be down from Harlem. He met Malik at the mosque he attended on Friday and he paid him 1000 a week to bust his gun. Today he was on his first mission and he was hiding under the stage the whole time.

"Sorry kid, no witnesses," she said, shooting him twice in his big head, splitting his skull.

"We out. I got him now. I want you to handle this shit," PYT told Red Hat.

They hopped in their cars, burning rubbing out the empty lot to see six empty vans parked.

***

Northeast, D.C.

Jalee and Hosayni both sat in his low-key apartment. She informed him that his pops was dead as well as his little brother and sister. He didn't really fuck with his mom Lipa, but she was still his mom.

Jalee was light-skinned, handsome, with waves, tats, hazel eyes, tall, chiseled, and a true gangsta. He was about getting money and no violence unless it was called for. At eighteen years old, he had his shit straight.

"I'm sorry, Jalee, but I had to come tell you," Hosayni said. She was dressed in regular jeans and a blouse with her hair in a long ponytail. She was beautiful. The two were close. Since she had been around, they had a crazy weird attraction.

"It's life. But I'ma handle it. Malik is still out there. I know he will get them. My mom trained us well. I'm jive like pissed slim ain't reach out to me. And how did you get down here, Hosayni?"

"I always know where you at, Jalee," she said, looking into his soft eyes.

"What's your plans? Now that my father is dead, where you going?" he asked her while keeping his emotions in control.

"I don't know. I have a lot of money from one of the hits. I guess I can go down south to live," she said.

"Marry me and we can move somewhere - Miami, Houston, Atlanta, wherever. I need you and I want you in my life," Jalee said. He had known she was the one for him for years.

"Yes, I'll marry you, Jalee," she said, kissing him.

One thing led to another. The two fucked all night until the morning. Jalee never had pussy so good. Hosayni was everything any man wished for and he had it.

The two went to a local mosque in D.C. and got married. Jalee had a couple of traps in the city. He planned to collect his money and never look back at the rough city he grew up in.

Chapter 35
Bronx, NY

Red Hat was sitting in his condo watching ESPN on his flat screen TV, but his mind was somewhere else.

The previous week's shootout did something to him. At the Empire meeting, nobody should have had the drop on them - unless it was an inside job, but he doubted that.

Thanks to PYT, they made it out on top. Twin was hit twice and had a punctured lung, but he was okay. He was planning a mean get-back. He was just waiting for everything to line up so he could make his next move.

"Yo Hat, the women have arrived," Big Milly said, holding a large remote with a camera built into the screen to see all his visitors coming in or going out.

"A'ight, Blood," Red Hat stated with a grin upon seeing Lyric and Yasmine walk into the lobby.

The women had been keeping tabs on Young Malik. There were a couple of things the young brother was into that was Harǔm (unlawful) in his deen. One was that he had drug shops throughout the tri-state area. Two, he had a very bad gambling problem. And three, he had a young white women that was seventeen years old whom he would pay for oral sex once or twice a week in Hunts Point, Bronx.

"Hey, papi, what you drinking?" Lyric asked, taking off her shoes. She stepped onto the Persian red rug in his living room. Yasmin was behind her, taking off her butter Timbs and sliding her iPhone into the back jeans pocket that hugged her phat ass.

"A little white Henny, babe. But what y'all got for daddy?" he said, kissing both of them on their lips as they took a seat next to him. They were happy to be home after a week of staking out Malik.

"Well…" Yasmine said with a long pause. "We been watching his every move, tailing him everywhere, and he rolls deep everywhere he goes," she said.

"Sometimes they play the cut, but rarely. They normally watching his every move. But there is one time throughout the week he is alone," Lyric said

"When?" Red Hat asked, hoping this info was a solid as what PYT told him.

"When he goes to see that young hooker bitch in Hunts Point, zaddy," Yasmine said, saying something he already knew.

"How often and what time does he go see the bitch? Y'all supposed to have more shit then this bullshit. I want to know where he rests, eats, and shits!" he shouted, getting upset.

"Papi, he moves around. He barely sleeps. He goes mosque to mosque. He moves like he knows we trying to kill him. He's very advanced, papi," Lyric said, being honest.

"He normally goes to see her on Tuesday and Sunday from 10:30-11:45 p.m. He takes the same route in the same car," Yasmine said, rubbing his thighs.

"A'ight, tonight, it's litty," he said, sipping out of his bottle.

Both women crawled between his legs, pulling his dick out of his Nike sweatsuit. They took turns sucking it slowly until he busted while they both played with his thick cum.

The three had a crazy threesome right there on the couch, taking turns doing every sexual position one could imagine from upside down anal and reverse cowgirl to a 69 position in the air.

***

Young Malik told his men to stay at the mosque because he had to meet his connect. They knew he would meet his connect every Sunday night - or so they thought.

Driving through certain parts of the Bronx at night was dangerous. Robbers were lurking and fiends were doing anything for a hit. There were shootouts and police killing black men, and little kids running around on bikes selling drugs.

Stopping at a red light, he saw a couple in their twenties arguing, about to fight. The police arrived right on time to see the male swing, knocking his girl out, then he swung on the police. Once they got him on the ground, they started kicking him in his face, knocking his teeth out.

Malik pushed his all-black Porsche Panamera with tints through south Bronx, the Hunts Point area, until he pulled up to Fox Lane, passing a White Castle fast food spot and a train station. Malik was still a virgin somewhat because he had never fucked a bitch. He just loved to get his dick sucked by white women because their blow jobs were out of this world.

Months ago he had seen a pretty brown woman standing around and she approached him, offering him the best blow job he would ever have, and he went for that. The woman took him in an alley and sucked his dick for two minutes and he nutted in her mouth. She swallowed everything.

When she told him the price, her voice changed from earlier and that fucked him up. Malik grabbed her pussy, only to feel a big dick under her dress.

The tranny told him that he was in the process of getting his dick cut and turned into a pussy, then he could get some pussy on the house.

Malik shot him in the head six times, then he vomited all over the alley. He had no clue she was a man because his ass and breasts were bigger than most women's.

He saw Lucy standing on the block with two older women trying to sell pussy. When she saw his Porsche, she walked over to him smiling.

Lucy was seventeen years old from upstate New York. She had run away from her group home and had been selling pussy, bouncing from pimp to pimp, shooting dope and living a fast life. She was 5'5", 127 pounds, blue eyes, long blonde hair, decent teeth, no ass, and flat breasts. She was very pretty, like Bella Hadid the model.

"Hey boo," Lucy said, climbing into the passenger seat as he parked behind a moving truck

"You okay? I missed you, and he did too," Malik said, pulling his dick out from under his garment.

Lucy smiled. She had ten minutes to report to her pimp Banger from Yonkers.

Lucy's head dove into his lap. She sucked the head, engulfing him up and down, slurping and spitting on it at the same time. She did tongue tricks on his pre-cum while bobbing up and down, wrapping her small thin lips around his dick as he moaned with his eyes closed.

Malik was so caught up that he never saw the shadows creeping up on him from both sides of his windows

Boom! Boom! Boom! Boom! Boom! Boom!

The loud sound erupted from the Glocks. Malik's and Lucy's necks were dripping blood and their heads dangled from their necks.

Red Hat and Yasmine hopped in the red Challenger coupe muscle car, pulling off. The good thing about Hunts Point was that nobody snitched because everybody was doing something illegal. When the police would come around, everybody would play dumb.

***

Cuba

Lately, everything had been coming back together, but Rugar still had some trials and tribulations he was facing.

Savannah was on her way over to pick up some items of her deceased mom's. He hadn't seen her since Hagor's funeral months ago. Rugar had a small meal cooked for her - a vegan dinner, because he knew she didn't eat meat.

"Sir, after your dinner, I have to talk to you about something very important," Valentina, the maid, said in her best English, placing a large bowl of salad on the dinner table as Savannah walked in.

Savannah walked into the dining room wearing a Versace embroidered sequin V-neck, showing her perfect breasts, barely covering the nipples. It was extra sexy.

"How's everything going? I called you to dinner to check on you. I don't even see you anymore. We still family," Rugar said trying to check her temperature because there was something off about her present.

"Oh, you check on me, just like you checked on my mom?" Savannah chuckled, then pulled out a large bottle of rum from her purse, taking a sip.

"What do you mean? I don't understand?"

"Don't you fucking play with me! I'm not stupid. I came here one day to check on my mom and say hi to you, then I heard her upstairs moaning, yelling, and screaming while you gave her everything I want!" she shouted with tears flowing. Savannah had seen everything from beginning to the end through the crack of the double doors. She hated the both of them after that scene.

"Savannah, I..." Rugar was at a loss for words.

"I saw you fucking her like you liked it. Why her and not me? Why am I not good enough? My pussy is tighter and better than that old bitch's. I'm still a virgin," she said, wiping her tears.

Rugar saw how crazy and insane she was.

"Answer me now!" she yelled. She slammed her glass bottle on the table, almost breaking it.

"I'm sorry," was all he could say.

"No sorry. There is only one way to fix it," she said, walking towards him. She sat on his lap and kissed his lips. He turned, but she snatched his head back to enjoy the kiss. She felt his hard dick and smiled brightly

"Thank you for the dinner. I'm sure you will make the right choice. Nobody has to know - unless you want people to know. We do look good together. I always get what I want, and I want you inside of me," she said as she walked off, swaying her hips. "Also, if you love your wife, you will follow my orders."

"You watch you fucking mouth, bitch! Don't ever threatening me or my wife!" he said, jumping up about to choke her

She stepped back, loving his madness.

"No, no, no, no, papi, I make no threats. The Cartel families are looking hard for my dear beautiful mother's murderer and we both know who did it," she said, fixing his tie making it straight as his face was ready to kill.

"I don't know what the fuck you talking about."

"Yes you do. I saw it with my own eyes. I have a safe room where I sometimes sleep, masturbate to you, or meditate. It's connected to the basement gym. The day my mom died, I watched the whole sword fight. My mom was a skillful sword fighter, papi, but PYT is the best I have ever seen. I could have helped. I hated my mom. PYT did me a favor and I got my mom's inheritance, so I'm set, and now I can, as you Americans say it, blackmail you," Savannah said.

"Fuck!" he yelled, punching the wall. He had no choice right now but to follow her rules. Killing her would be too risky and would lead the cartel families to do a full investigation, which could lead back to him or PYT.

"See you later, papi," Savannah said, walking out the front door like a true diva.

Rugar walked out back to get some fresh air and saw the maid staring into the empty field

"You okay, sir? I heard lots of screaming," the maid said softly, hoping he was okay because she liked Rugar.

"Yes, everything is fine. But what do you have to talk about?" he asked, walking into the field, going for a walk as she walked along his side.

"I know this isn't the perfect time to tell you this, but I saw who killed Hagor. I just come in to work and I saw her," the maid said.

"Are you sure? Because I heard nobody was here," he replied, hoping she would change her mind.

"Sir, I saw her with my own eyes," she said, stepping on dirt and rocks.

"Who was it?" he asked.

She gave him an awkward look as if he wasn't going to believe it. "Your wife, sir," she said sharply.

"Who did you tell this to?" he asked.

"You're the first, sir. I'm sorry, but I had to tell you, sir. Your wife is a dangerous women," the maid stated.

"Yeah, I'm sorry too," Rugar said, pulling out a pistol and shooting her in the side of her head, leaving her body under some grapevines. Rugar walked back to the house and told another maid to go into the field and dispose of the body and that whoever else stole from him would be buried with her old ass.

Chapter 36
Months later

The last couple of months had been quiet in the city. The Muslims were out of the picture for good. Malik had been the last man standing strong before Red Hat killed him, but they all respected the fight in the dog.

PYT sat in her Port Chester mansion, watching the winter snowfall from the sky in her driveway from her living room with the fireplace light, drinking coffee. She felt better now that the beef was over. Now she could regain the streets without looking over her shoulders 24/7.

Rugar was coming home in a day or so and she wanted to plan something special for her husband. She knew he was busy getting the new product out to the cartel families. She missed every piece of him and his presence. Brandon was having a weekend sleepover with his best friend from school.

PYT was also in touch with China daily. She recently got an internship at a law firm in Miami. She was doing well. The Empire was doing great. Everybody was doing them, living life, balling hard, and banging harder.

The only thing that didn't sit well with her was the cartels dealing with the Hagor situation. She only hoped it would blow over in due time.

The vibration of her cell phone startled her. It was a text from Rugar, informing her that he was on his way early. She smiled like a kid at prom. Every time she got around him, their love felt brand new. An hour later, Rugar pulled up in his new all-white Bentley truck followed by a truck full of goons - six of them.

"Take off, but come back in the morning. I have a meeting at 10 a.m. And Big World? Please don't shoot nobody tonight at a strip club, because I'm not bailing you out," Rugar said, grabbing his Gucci suitcase.

"Okay, boss, buenas noches," the big man said, climbing in the passenger seat, pulling off, ready to get drunk and grab some ass in one of the exotic strip clubs in New York.

***

PYT had just gotten out of the shower. She wore only a Chanel silk robe and heels. She was naked underneath, ready to get fucked. She planned to rock his world tonight.

She walked out of her bedroom. Her high heels slowly clicked on the marble tiles, making a tapping noise. The house was too silent. She figured Rugar was either in the kitchen or in his office planning something romantic.

As she got a little closer to his office door, she saw it cracked, which was odd because Rugar always closed it. What made her alert was the noise. It sounded as if someone was mumbling or moaning in a "help me" way.

PYT covered up her exposed breasts and then pulled out a pistol from her thigh holster, something she carried around daily. She creeped on the wall, aimed her gun, and busted into the room with her heart racing

"Zeema, put it down," a strong African voice said firmly. She started to tremble as she looked at the familiar face of her Uncle Zebemen.

"Let him go first," she said while looking at her husband tied to a chair with duct tape wrapped around his mouth.

Zebemen had sneaked into the house after he disable the alarm. He followed Rugar to his office and choked him out and then tied him up. Zebemen was a very big man at 6'6" and very strong, also a skilled fighter, like most of his tribal men. Not to mention he had two of his men with him standing there with long jungle swords, dressed in suits like him to blend in with the Americans.

"Nice to see you again. It's been a while. I was just explaining to this guy who is supposed to be your husband how you were supposed to come back home years ago. That was the deal your mother and father had. Fifteen years in Africa, five in the States, then fifteen more in Africa, then you'd be a free women. But you broke the contract," Zebemen said with a blade at Rugar's neck.

"I'm not going back. Before I get mad, let him go," she said, making everyone laugh.

"Yes, you are. Your father wants you back in seventy-two hours. They need you to take your position within the family. If not, the grim reaper will be looking for you, and I'm sure none of us wants that. And she hunts to kill - especially you," her uncle said.

"Let him go. I'll be there," she said, seeing the blade starting to make him bleed.

"Okay, my niece. I gave you my orders. My brother isn't pleased," he said, walking towards her. She still had her gun cocked and aimed.

"Don't come too close or I'll blow your ugly ass up," she stated.

"I admire your work, but you got a lot more work to do to catch up. She is taking hits. You're supposed to be with her, but instead, you play housewife," he said, smiling, now face to face with her. "We don't use guns in our country. We use swords: quick, quiet, and easy," he said, staring into the barrel of her gun.

"Well, over here we use guns: faster, quicker, and a guaranteed kill," she said as the windows busted open.

Psst! Psst! Psst! Psst! Psst! Psst!

The two guards dropped as the silent bullets killed them both. Zebemen looked towards the windows, backing up with his sword. Within seconds, bullets ripped through his skull, making his head jerk backwards twice as he fell face first into an oak table next to Rugar's laptop.

PYT ducked and rushed to untie Rugar with her pistol ready to bust because there was a sniper nearby.

"Fuck, we gotta get out of here," Rugar said, grabbing his pistol from the drawer. They rushed to the door, but before they exited, a thick zip line was shot into the wall. Then a man dressed in all black used the line to land in the office.

As soon as he stood up, both of their guns were trained on him.

"I love to zip line. But don't shoot," the handsome man said, lifting his hands in the air. He had a big special made sniper assault rifle hanging from his neck. The men was Spanish. He had a goatee and long hair in a ponytail. He was in shape and had light skin and hazel eyes. He looked to be in his early 50's.

"Who the fuck are you and what's going on?" Rugar asked, ready to shoot

"I'm Black Mist, a Cuban legend. I was sent to watch over you both. I'm like a hidden angel. Nice to meet you both. PYT, I'm a fan of your work. A lot of people speak highly of you. But I have to go," Black Mist said, leaving the same way he came in, leaving glass and bodies in his wake.

He had been posted on top of the guest house. He knew everything about Zebemen and the dangerous vicious tribe and king. So when he came to New York, Black Mist did also. He owed Jumbo his life and he promised him he would look out for Rugar.

Hagor was his sister, but the two were like night and day. They really hated each other. When she recently died, he didn't even shed a tear. He couldn't if he tried.

"That's rude. He is a famous assassin. He just saved our lives. But we have to get going. Come on. Brandon is safe for now," PYT said as they rushed out the house with three important suitcases full of money and documents with weapons.

PYT called Red Hat and told him to pick up Lil Brazy and play daddy daycare until she could figure some shit out. When he tried to ask what happened she said, "World War 3," then hung up.

***

They were driving downtown to lay low in a hotel, but PYT told him to go to her low-key condo nobody know about - not even him.

"I won't let them take you or what we built. I'm ready for war. I'ma protect you," Rugar said, knowing most of the time she was the one saving his ass. But he was willing to put his life on the line for her anytime of the day.

"This is a different type of war, love, a war I'ma having to face myself," she said, knowing he wouldn't really understand. When she was younger, PYT sold her soul to the devil and evil spirts. Her father made her do it because it was in her tribal bloodline to do so.

"We die together. You talking crazy right now, baby," he said, getting off the expressway to her condo as she directed him.

***

One month later

The two had been in the downtown condo plotting, planning, networking, and making love. There were guards on rooftops, downstairs in another condo, and parked out front. Rugar was taking no chances.

PYT explained to him everything about her past, her blood-line, her sacrifices, and selling her soul to demons.

"I'ma go meet up with some important people who have connections to your father. Did you know he controls the heroin trade in South and West Africa?" Rugar asked.

"Yes, I did know, and he wants me and my sister to take over since we're his only kids and he can't make anymore. He wanted boys, but got two girls, so that's why he trained us the way he did: to turn us into boys. His brother wanted him to kill us, but my father refused. I haven't seen my mother since a baby. When I came to the States, I stayed with my aunty and Naya," said PYT, watching him get dressed

"Baby, don't worry. I'ma do everything in my power to have your ties cut trust me money talks," Rugar said, putting on his Rolex watch.

"It's not about the money, babe," she said, getting out of bed in her pajamas to take a shower and get some more sleep. They had a long night last night. That was her second time trying anal with him and it hurt so bad, she tapped out.

Rugar kissed her and left while she took a shower and took a nap.

***
Two hours later

PYT was sound asleep, snoring lightly, deep in her dreams. She was a hard sleeper because she was on alert all day.

There was a loud cough that woke her up. Once she clearly gained her vision, she jumped up, only to be knocked back down by a huge Chinese guard. There were thirteen Chinese men with guns pointed at her and one man standing in front of her short in a suit. He looked like Jackie Chan, but smaller.

"Jasmine, good to see you again. I'm sure you remember me," Mr. Hubei of the China Cartel stated, smiling.

"What do you want?" she said, feeling for her thigh pistol.

"Your weapons are all gone. You sleep very hard. My men wanted to rape you, but we don't do that in our country. But where you're going...that's a different story," he said, laughing.

PYT knew there was no way she could fight her way out of this one. It was useless if she wanted to stay alive.

"Why are you doing this? I'm a part of the Cartel Commission. You're going against your oath. I wonder what the other families will say?" PYT said.

He laughed and talked in Chinese to his men, making them laugh also.

"That's business. This is personal. For one, I know you killed Hagor. I had cameras set up in her basement gym for years because there was a point where I thought she was a CIA agent, but I was wrong," he said.

PYT felt dumb and hopeless. "So just kill me get it over with," she said.

"I wish I could, but I'm not only here about Hagor. I couldn't care less about her. She was only a good fuck. But the rest... I'll let them answer it for you," he said, sticking her with a needle.

"Who?" she said as her body went numb and she passed out. Again, this scene looked too familiar to her.

Hours later, she woke up in a cage with two other women with kids, naked just like her. She knew she was on a train, but to where? She felt her private parts to make sure she hadn't been raped.

She went over to the two women, who looked younger than her and scared. She could tell the pretty women were either Liberian or Guyanese. Luckily she spoke Guyanese, Creole, and Amerindian. PYT asked the women where they were in both languages and they just looked at each other, not understanding.

"We speak English," one of them said.

"Good. Oh my God, what the fuck is going on? Why are we here?" PYT said.

"Shhhh! Be quiet or they will kill you. We don't know where we are going, but wherever it is, I can tell you it's not good," one of them said.

"Who will kill us?" PYT asked.

"The same people who killed them," the other female said, holding her starving baby and pointing to the next cage over to see over twenty dead bodies of kids and females.

PYT sat down in fetal position, trying not to cry, but she know this was karma for all the people she had killed with no remorse. The only person she could think about was Rugar.

"Psssssst! Go to sleep, or fake sleep. If they see you awake, they will try to kill you. They're coming," one of the women, said closing her eyes then snoring as if she was really asleep.

PYT did the same. She placed her head in her legs and faked sleep as she heard footsteps, but no voices. Before the men walked, out there was a woman's voice she heard that made her blood boil. Now she knew where she was and who was behind this and the tears rolled down her legs...

To Be Continued...
Gangland Cartel 3
Coming Soon

Submission Guideline

Submit the first three chapters of your completed manuscript to ldpsubmissions@gmail.com, subject line: Your book's title. The manuscript must be in a .doc file and sent as an attachment. Document should be in Times New Roman, double spaced and in size 12 font. Also, provide your synopsis and full contact information. If sending multiple submissions, they must each be in a separate email.

Have a story but no way to send it electronically? You can still submit to LDP/Ca$h Presents. Send in the first three chapters, written or typed, of your completed manuscript to:

LDP: Submissions Dept
Po Box 944
Stockbridge, Ga 30281

DO NOT send original manuscript. Must be a duplicate.

Provide your synopsis and a cover letter containing your full contact information.

Thanks for considering LDP and Ca$h Presents.

Coming Soon from Lock Down Publications/Ca$h Presents

BOW DOWN TO MY GANGSTA

By **Ca$h**

TORN BETWEEN TWO

By **Coffee**

THE STREETS STAINED MY SOUL **II**

By **Marcellus Allen**

BLOOD OF A BOSS **VI**

SHADOWS OF THE GAME II

By **Askari**

LOYAL TO THE GAME **IV**

By **T.J. & Jelissa**

IF LOVING YOU IS WRONG… **III**

By **Jelissa**

TRUE SAVAGE **VII**

MIDNIGHT CARTEL III

DOPE BOY MAGIC IV

CITY OF KINGZ II

By **Chris Green**

BLAST FOR ME **III**

A SAVAGE DOPEBOY III

CUTTHROAT MAFIA III

By **Ghost**

A HUSTLER'S DECEIT III

KILL ZONE **II**

BAE BELONGS TO ME III

A DOPE BOY'S QUEEN III

By **Aryanna**

COKE KINGS V

KING OF THE TRAP II
By **T.J. Edwards**
GORILLAZ IN THE BAY V
3X KRAZY II
De'Kari
THE STREETS ARE CALLING II
Duquie Wilson
KINGPIN KILLAZ IV
STREET KINGS III
PAID IN BLOOD III
CARTEL KILLAZ IV
DOPE GODS III
Hood Rich
SINS OF A HUSTLA II
ASAD
KINGZ OF THE GAME VI
Playa Ray
SLAUGHTER GANG IV
RUTHLESS HEART IV
By Willie Slaughter
THE HEART OF A SAVAGE III
By Jibril Williams
FUK SHYT II
By Blakk Diamond
THE REALEST KILLAZ III
By Tranay Adams
TRAP GOD III
By Troublesome
YAYO IV
GHOST MOB

Stilloan Robinson

KINGPIN DREAMS III

By Paper Boi Rari

CREAM II

By Yolanda Moore

SON OF A DOPE FIEND III

By Renta

FOREVER GANGSTA II

GLOCKS ON SATIN SHEETS III

By Adrian Dulan

LOYALTY AIN'T PROMISED III

By Keith Williams

THE PRICE YOU PAY FOR LOVE II

By Destiny Skai

CONFESSIONS OF A GANGSTA III

By Nicholas Lock

I'M NOTHING WITHOUT HIS LOVE II

SINS OF A THUG II

By Monet Dragun

LIFE OF A SAVAGE IV

A GANGSTA'S QUR'AN III

MURDA SEASON III

GANGLAND CARTEL III

By **Romell Tukes**

QUIET MONEY III

THUG LIFE II

By **Trai'Quan**

THE STREETS MADE ME III

By **Larry D. Wright**

THE ULTIMATE SACRIFICE VI

IF YOU CROSS ME ONCE II

ANGEL III

By **Anthony Fields**

FRIEND OR FOE III

By **Mimi**

SAVAGE STORMS II

By **Meesha**

BLOOD ON THE MONEY II

By J-Blunt

THE STREETS WILL NEVER CLOSE II

By K'ajji

NIGHTMARES OF A HUSTLA II

By King Dream

THE WIFEY I USED TO BE II

By Nicole Goosby

IN THE ARM OF HIS BOSS

By Jamila

<u>Available Now</u>

RESTRAINING ORDER **I & II**

By **CA$H & Coffee**

LOVE KNOWS NO BOUNDARIES **I II & III**

By **Coffee**

RAISED AS A GOON I, II, III & IV

BRED BY THE SLUMS I, II, III

BLAST FOR ME I & II

ROTTEN TO THE CORE I II III

A BRONX TALE I, II, III

DUFFEL BAG CARTEL I II III IV

HEARTLESS GOON I II III IV
A SAVAGE DOPEBOY I II
HEARTLESS GOON I II III
DRUG LORDS I II III
CUTTHROAT MAFIA I II
By **Ghost**
LAY IT DOWN **I & II**
LAST OF A DYING BREED
BLOOD STAINS OF A SHOTTA I & II III
By **Jamaica**
LOYAL TO THE GAME I II III
LIFE OF SIN I, II III
By **TJ & Jelissa**
BLOODY COMMAS I & II
SKI MASK CARTEL I II & III
KING OF NEW YORK I II,III IV V
RISE TO POWER I II III
COKE KINGS I II III IV
BORN HEARTLESS I II III IV
KING OF THE TRAP
By **T.J. Edwards**
IF LOVING HIM IS WRONG…I & II
LOVE ME EVEN WHEN IT HURTS I II III
By **Jelissa**
WHEN THE STREETS CLAP BACK I & II III
THE HEART OF A SAVAGE I II
By **Jibril Williams**
A DISTINGUISHED THUG STOLE MY HEART I II & III
LOVE SHOULDN'T HURT I II III IV
RENEGADE BOYS I II III IV

PAID IN KARMA I II III

SAVAGE STORMS

By **Meesha**

A GANGSTER'S CODE I &, II III

A GANGSTER'S SYN I II III

THE SAVAGE LIFE I II III

CHAINED TO THE STREETS I II III

BLOOD ON THE MONEY

By J-Blunt

PUSH IT TO THE LIMIT

By **Bre' Hayes**

BLOOD OF A BOSS **I, II, III, IV, V**

SHADOWS OF THE GAME

By **Askari**

THE STREETS BLEED MURDER **I, II & III**

THE HEART OF A GANGSTA I II& III

By **Jerry Jackson**

CUM FOR ME I II III IV V VI

An **LDP Erotica Collaboration**

BRIDE OF A HUSTLA **I II & II**

THE FETTI GIRLS **I, II& III**

CORRUPTED BY A GANGSTA I, II III, IV

BLINDED BY HIS LOVE

THE PRICE YOU PAY FOR LOVE

DOPE GIRL MAGIC I II III

By **Destiny Skai**

WHEN A GOOD GIRL GOES BAD

By **Adrienne**

THE COST OF LOYALTY I II III

By Kweli

A GANGSTER'S REVENGE **I II III & IV**

THE BOSS MAN'S DAUGHTERS I II III IV V

A SAVAGE LOVE **I & II**

BAE BELONGS TO ME I II

A HUSTLER'S DECEIT I, II, III

WHAT BAD BITCHES DO I, II, III

SOUL OF A MONSTER I II III

KILL ZONE

A DOPE BOY'S QUEEN I II

By **Aryanna**

A KINGPIN'S AMBITON

A KINGPIN'S AMBITION **II**

I MURDER FOR THE DOUGH

By **Ambitious**

TRUE SAVAGE I II III IV V VI

DOPE BOY MAGIC I, II, III

MIDNIGHT CARTEL I II

CITY OF KINGZ

By **Chris Green**

A DOPEBOY'S PRAYER

By **Eddie "Wolf" Lee**

THE KING CARTEL **I, II & III**

By **Frank Gresham**

THESE NIGGAS AIN'T LOYAL **I, II & III**

By **Nikki Tee**

GANGSTA SHYT **I II &III**

By **CATO**

THE ULTIMATE BETRAYAL

By **Phoenix**

BOSS'N UP **I , II & III**

By **Royal Nicole**
I LOVE YOU TO DEATH
By Destiny J
I RIDE FOR MY HITTA
I STILL RIDE FOR MY HITTA
By **Misty Holt**
LOVE & CHASIN' PAPER
By **Qay Crockett**
TO DIE IN VAIN
SINS OF A HUSTLA
By **ASAD**
BROOKLYN HUSTLAZ
By **Boogsy Morina**
BROOKLYN ON LOCK I & II
By **Sonovia**
GANGSTA CITY
By **Teddy Duke**
A DRUG KING AND HIS DIAMOND I & II III
A DOPEMAN'S RICHES
HER MAN, MINE'S TOO I, II
CASH MONEY HO'S
THE WIFEY I USED TO BE
By Nicole Goosby
TRAPHOUSE KING **I II & III**
KINGPIN KILLAZ I II III
STREET KINGS I II
PAID IN BLOOD **I II**
CARTEL KILLAZ I II III
DOPE GODS I II
By **Hood Rich**

LIPSTICK KILLAH **I, II, III**

CRIME OF PASSION I II & III

FRIEND OR FOE I II

By **Mimi**

STEADY MOBBN' **I, II, III**

THE STREETS STAINED MY SOUL

By **Marcellus Allen**

WHO SHOT YA **I, II, III**

SON OF A DOPE FIEND I II

Renta

GORILLAZ IN THE BAY **I II III IV**

TEARS OF A GANGSTA I II

3X KRAZY

DE'KARI

TRIGGADALE I II III

Elijah R. Freeman

GOD BLESS THE TRAPPERS I, II, III

THESE SCANDALOUS STREETS I, II, III

FEAR MY GANGSTA I, II, III IV, V

THESE STREETS DON'T LOVE NOBODY I, II

BURY ME A G I, II, III, IV, V

A GANGSTA'S EMPIRE I, II, III, IV

THE DOPEMAN'S BODYGAURD I II

THE REALEST KILLAZ I II

Tranay Adams

THE STREETS ARE CALLING

Duquie Wilson

MARRIED TO A BOSS... I II III

By Destiny Skai & Chris Green

KINGZ OF THE GAME I II III IV V

Playa Ray
SLAUGHTER GANG I II III
RUTHLESS HEART I II III
By Willie Slaughter
FUK SHYT
By Blakk Diamond
DON'T F#CK WITH MY HEART I II
By Linnea
ADDICTED TO THE DRAMA I II III
IN THE ARM OF HIS BOSS II
By Jamila
YAYO I II III
A SHOOTER'S AMBITION I II
By S. Allen
TRAP GOD I II
By Troublesome
FOREVER GANGSTA
GLOCKS ON SATIN SHEETS I II
By Adrian Dulan
TOE TAGZ I II III
By Ah'Million
KINGPIN DREAMS I II
By Paper Boi Rari
CONFESSIONS OF A GANGSTA I II
By Nicholas Lock
I'M NOTHING WITHOUT HIS LOVE
SINS OF A THUG
By Monet Dragun
CAUGHT UP IN THE LIFE I II III
By Robert Baptiste

NEW TO THE GAME I II III

By **Malik D. Rice**

LIFE OF A SAVAGE I II III

A GANGSTA'S QUR'AN I II

MURDA SEASON I II

GANGLAND CARTEL I II

By **Romell Tukes**

LOYALTY AIN'T PROMISED I II

By Keith Williams

QUIET MONEY I II

THUG LIFE

By **Trai'Quan**

THE STREETS MADE ME I II

By **Larry D. Wright**

THE ULTIMATE SACRIFICE I, II, III, IV, V

KHADIFI

IF YOU CROSS ME ONCE

ANGEL I II

By **Anthony Fields**

THE LIFE OF A HOOD STAR

By Ca$h & Rashia Wilson

THE STREETS WILL NEVER CLOSE

By K'ajji

CREAM

By Yolanda Moore

NIGHTMARES OF A HUSTLA

By King Dream

BOOKS BY LDP'S CEO, CA$H

TRUST IN NO MAN

TRUST IN NO MAN 2

TRUST IN NO MAN 3

BONDED BY BLOOD

SHORTY GOT A THUG

THUGS CRY

THUGS CRY 2

THUGS CRY 3

TRUST NO BITCH

TRUST NO BITCH 2

TRUST NO BITCH 3

TIL MY CASKET DROPS

RESTRAINING ORDER

RESTRAINING ORDER 2

IN LOVE WITH A CONVICT

LIFE OF A HOOD STAR

www.ingramcontent.com/pod-product-compliance
Lightning Source LLC
Chambersburg PA
CBHW070511260626
47161CB00004B/1517